PAULA DANZIGER

DELACORTE PRESS/NEW YORK

Published by
Delacorte Press
1 Dag Hammarskjold Plaza
New York, New York   10017

"GIVE MY REGARDS TO BROADWAY" (George M.
Cohan)
Used by permission of GEORGE M. COHAN MUSIC
PUBLISHING COMPANY.

Manufactured in the United States of America

First printing

Library of Congress Cataloging in Publication Data

Danziger, Paula [date of birth]
    Remember me to Harold Square.

    Summary: When Frank spends the summer with Kendra and
her family in their New York City apartment, a friendship devel-
ops as the two teenagers set off on a scavenger hunt exploring the
city's museums, restaurants, and other landmarks.
    [1. Friendship—Fiction. 2. New York (N.Y.)—Description
and travel—Fiction] I. Title.
PZ7.D2394Re 1987   [Fic]   87-6844
ISBN 0-385-29610-X

To my "kid" brother and his family,
Barry, Annette, Sam'l, Carrie,
and "Mr. Ben" Danziger

ACKNOWLEDGMENTS

For listening to the process:
Ann Farber, June Foley, Pat Giff, Sue Haven, Francine
Pascal, Melita Horvat-Stupack, Jane Traum

For telling me about growing up in New York City:
Susan Pascal Johansson, Elyse Myller

For exploring New York City with me:
Tina Canales, Paul Haven,
Bill, Carol, Bill Jr., Rachel and Chuck Lindsay,
Ellen Teguis

For making research as easy as ABC:
Donna Larson

For a great cover:
Joe Csatari, artist; Jerry Counihan, art director

For editing above and beyond the call of duty:
Lori Mack

"Kendra, if you don't vacuum in here soon, we're going to have to start giving names to the dust balls," my mother says, looking around my bedroom.

"Mom, you promised not to nag me about my room and sarcasm definitely counts as nagging." I take a sock off the doorknob. "Remember the deal—I can keep the room the way that I want, except for the bed, as long as the clutter doesn't spread to any of the other rooms."

She sighs. "I don't know how you ever convinced your father and me to agree to this."

Looking under my bed for the matching sock, I keep my head under there for a minute to get some peace and quiet.

She continues anyway. "It would be so nice to see your carpet."

"Mom, you promised." I stand up and pretend to rearrange some papers on my desk. "Anyway, I'm cleaning up my room, right now, of my own free will."

"That's because you have two days to straighten up this disaster area for your pajama party, so that your friends have room to put down sleeping bags and so that Bethany doesn't have an allergy attack."

She's got me.

I say nothing.

It's true.

Can I help it if my best friend is allergic to dust mites?

Fortunately, she changes the subject. "Kendra, tell me honestly. Was last night's party well chaperoned?"

Unfortunately, she's changed it to another subject designed to drive me crazy.

"Mom, you've asked me that five million times. And I've told you five million times that it was just a party to celebrate the end of ninth grade and the beginning of summer vacation. Teri's mother, father, six-year-old brother, and her fourteen-year-old cocker spaniel were there. So were the goldfish in the tank—although there had been a rumor that they would be going out to see a double feature of *Jaws* and *Piranha*."

"Young lady." My mother smiles. "Don't tease me. You know that I'm a worrier. I just want my family to be safe."

Worrier is an understatement.

"Call Mrs. Watson and check with her," I continue. "Teri invited no muggers, no perverts, and no bad B-O-Y-S. Your only daughter was safe. Mom, you used to be a class mother. You've known most of these kids since I was in preschool. Stop worrying."

She sighs.

My mother sighs so much that I tell her that her reaction to whatever I do is "one sighs fits all."

She tells me that my attempts at independence are a way of my "trying it on for sighs."

"Kendra. We have to be so careful nowadays. All of the terrible things that I read about in the papers. . . . I just want you to be careful."

I throw some of my old notebooks into the wastepaper basket. They have some of last year's notes in them but are mostly filled with doodles. I'm a good student but definitely not a scholar. "Mom. I'm fourteen years old—practically a grown-up. If we lived in a primitive society, I would probably be married with kids at this age."

"New York City is not a primitive society," my mother says softly. "And I hope you're not doing anything that will lead to marriage or kids—not in the near future."

It's my turn to sigh. "I don't even have a boyfriend right now. Please let up."

"If I had ever told my parents to let up, I wouldn't have been allowed out of my room for years." She picks up my pair of earrings, holds them up to her ears, looks at the mirror, makes a face, and puts them back down. "Honey, don't make things hard for me. I just want my family to be safe."

"Mom. I'm fourteen. I'm not a baby anymore," I remind her.

"You're not an adult yet—and anyway, you'll always be my child."

Ugh. Yuck. Phooey. She's driving me nuts. That's one of the major problems in my life. My parents want to treat me like a kid and I want to be more of an adult

—except when I want to be treated like a kid, and then they tell me to act more like a grown-up. Life is so confusing and such a pain sometimes.

I bet that when my hundredth birthday is announced on the *Today* show, my mother will go on and tell them that my room is still a mess and that the reason I'm a hundred is that she's kept me safe—bored but safe.

My father says I should be more understanding.

I do try to be more understanding. I know the facts.

My mother's parents were in the Holocaust. That was during World War II, the awful time when people were put in concentration camps and often tortured and killed. My grandparents managed to get out alive, but my dad says that what happened to them affected my mother, even though she was born years later in the United States.

So I really do try to be more understanding—kind of look out for my mother and do what she says—but sometimes it's really hard to deal with.

Today is definitely one of those days.

"Kendra." My mother looks at my room. "I'm going to go and do some of the laundry. When I finish, I'll stop back here to see if you've located the floor yet."

"I'm sure it's here somewhere." I go back under the bed to see if more articles of clothing have strayed there.

She leaves and I look around my room.

I'm always making promises to myself to be neater, but it never seems to work. If ceilings were made of

Velcro, I would just throw stuff up there and use a pole to knock it down when needed.

My parents are always saying that it's a mystery how I find anything in my messy room.

I've explained my system to them many times but they never seem to understand.

The dirty clothes go mostly into a pile in the bottom of my closet, in the right corner of my bedroom, and under the bed.

As for the bed, it's perfectly made because of a bet. My mother said I would do badly on a research paper that I did the night before it was due. I said that I'd get at least a B—, since Mr. Johns never seems to read the papers anyway. Mr. Johns got sick and the school got a sub who actually majored in the subject. She gave me a C, and now I have to make the bed for two more months. My mother says that she hopes it taught me a lesson about doing my work at the last minute. What it taught me was never to bet with my mother.

There are novels all over the floor and under the bed since I never like to be too far from a book.

Jewelry is on wall hooks so everything can be looked at, even when not being worn.

My stuffed animals are on the top of the dresser. So are special memory things like my first baby tooth, a spelling medal from the third grade, and pictures of my class from preschool through ninth grade. It may seem kind of sentimental to some people but I really like my school and most of the kids in it. Going to a small private school in New York City, you get to know everyone pretty well and share a lot of experiences. Like the time the gym teacher took us to Central Park to play hockey and some guys tried to mug us. We beat them off with our hockey sticks. Stuff like that can make people pretty close.

That's why the party was fun but also kind of sad. It was hard saying good-bye to so many people who are going away for the whole summer.

Since I'm one of the few people who is going to be staying in the City, I've decided to have a pajama party. It's the last chance for all of the girls to get together before everyone gets involved in summer plans. And since my social life (as in B-O-Y-S) is practically nonexistent and not likely to change over the summer, I figured it would be fun to have a pajama party, which is something we haven't done in a long time. We thought about having a co-ed one, but my parents said *absolutely not.*

I rearrange the stuff on my dresser, trying, as my mother always says, "to make order out of disorder." Stuff like that is probably important to people like her, but not as important to people like me.

I wipe the dust off the picture of me with Jeremy, the guy I used to date before we decided that ours was not destined to be the love of the century, or even of the marking period. I like the picture, though, so it's still on the dresser.

I look at the picture and then at my reflection in the mirror.

Four months have not made a big difference in my looks. My eyes are still blue. My hair is still brown, with sort of natural red highlights in it. There are still these freckles across my nose and face that Jeremy said were "cute" and that I think look like a permanent case of chicken pox.

I'm probably not as flat-chested as I was then, but it's hard to tell, since I like to wear really loose-fitting clothes.

My mother sticks her head back in the door. "Honey, are the rest of your dirty clothes ready to go into the washing machine?"

I gather the piles up, put them into a huge garbage bag, and drag it over to her.

She looks at it. "Is that all yours or have you taken in laundry to supplement the allowance that you are always complaining is so small?"

I grin at her. "It's all mine, except for a few things that I borrowed."

"Like my new blouse, which has been missing for several weeks." She pulls it off the top of the pile. "Kendra, this is supposed to be hand washed. If you're going to borrow my clothes, you have to take better care of them."

"OK." I stick another top into the bag.

"I never noticed that one before," she says.

I pull it out again and hold it up. "It's a *Brady Bunch* T-shirt. See? Here are pictures of Marsha and Cindy and Jan. I traded it for my "You've got to have Park" T-shirt that I got at the concert last summer."

She frowns. "I'm not sure that your father's going to be pleased to see you with something that has to do with television. You know how he feels about most shows."

I shove the shirt back into the bag and pick up the Dustbuster. I begin vacuuming the stuffed animals so that I don't have to listen.

As she leaves, she gives the room one of those looks that need no words—but I know what she's thinking.

Finishing with the Dustbuster, I take one of my ancient T-shirts and use it to clean my butterfly collection, which is right next to my Venus's flytraps on the windowsill.

The oldest butterfly was given to me on the date of my birth by my father, and ever since then I've been collecting them.

Butterflies. I wonder if they get anxiety attacks when they have to leave the cocoon, even if they really do want to go.

Think about it. It's got to be rough. One minute you're this little creepy-crawler used to slithering along the ground, trying not to get stepped on, and then you go into a cocoon and come out a changed worm. No more slithering, no more having to look up at everything. You have a different body that you're not sure what to do with.

Worms and kids have a lot in common. Just as soon as you get used to things being one way, you turn into something else—a butterfly or what books refer to as "a young adult."

Personally, if I were a caterpillar, I'd hate to leave the cocoon.

Just as I am thinking about worms, my little brother walks in.

"Knock!" I yell.

"The door's open. I have to walk in to knock." He sticks his tongue out at me.

I bet that the Dustbuster could handle his tongue.

"Oscar, what do you want?" I stare at him.

"What I want is to be an only child," he says.

I wonder whether his beady little head would fit in a Dustbuster.

"Dad's making lunch and said I had to find out what you want to eat," the creep informs me.

I tell him. "Ham and cheese with lettuce, mustard on one side, mayo on the other, with pickle slices on the cheese side and ruffled potato chips on the other side."

"That's disgusting." He makes a face.

"So are you."

Exiting, he says, "I'll tell Dad that you want dog-do-shish-kabob."

My parents say it's a mystery that Oscar and I haven't murdered each other yet.

I tend to agree.

What can be said about a ten-year-old brother named Oscar Kaye, who goes around saying, "I'm O.K. and you're not." Who every adult thinks is "charming," who has genius test scores, who keeps bugging his sister—me, Kendra Kaye—by saying, "I'm O.K. and you're K.K.," making my initials sound like he's retching.

It's not easy having a younger brother like him and it's not going to get any easier.

School's over and we can't afford to go away to

camp, or travel, or have a country home like many kids at our school do.

We do not, as my father says, have a money tree growing in our backyard.

Since my mother is a librarian and my father is a professor at a college in the suburbs, we are not one of the city's wealthiest families. We do not even have a money *bush* growing in our backyard.

Furthermore, since we live in an apartment building, we don't even have any trees in our backyard. We don't even have a backyard.

And because neither Oscar nor I want to go to day camp, we're going to be spending a lot of time together.

The mystery is how I'm going to survive the summer.

"Kids. We have a surprise for you," my father announces at the dining room table.

"We've won the lottery." Oscar claps his hands. "Now we can go to Disneyland. Now we can buy Disneyland."

"No," my mother says. "We did not win the lottery, and if we had won, there are many places that we would go before Disneyland—places with a real sense of history."

"Disneyland's got a history. It's older than I am. Mickey Mouse has even got a song." Oscar starts singing.

My father stuffs a spoonful of mashed potatoes in the kid's mouth.

That doesn't stop Oscar. He finishes the song with the mashed potatoes sort of dribbling out of his mouth and then says, "Another guess. You've decided to let us watch as much television as we want."

"Not a chance." My father takes a napkin, ties two knots, and pretends that the napkin is a rabbit puppet.

He's been doing that for as long as I've known him.

It's really goofy.

I wonder if somewhere in the United States there are people who sit down at a table and just eat a normal meal.

The rabbit puppet talks in a high-pitched voice. (My father's lips always move.) "You know that you watch too much television. The rule is five hours a week for each of you. And you can't say five hours for Oscar plus five hours for Kendra with each watching the other's TV. Also, don't forget, no television-watching during the day."

Why does Oscar have to mention TV? He knows the rules. We promised that we'd follow them if we didn't have to go to boring day camp. We made a deal with my parents, and once a deal is made, they don't relent.

"You'll never guess." The bunny "bites" Oscar on the nose.

I only like surprises when I know what they are and when I know that it's something that I'm going to like.

Being older than Oscar means knowing more about my parents' ways. Sometimes their surprises are great —like the trip to Williamsburg, Virginia, in the fourth grade and like giving me riding lessons in sixth grade.

Sometimes the surprises are things like "Surprise. You have a baby brother" or "Surprise. You're going to summer school to study shorthand" or "Surprise. We're having tuna melt casserole tonight."

So I wait.

"You're going to buy me a skateboard." Oscar claps his hands again.

"Never," says my mother.

Shut up, Oscar, I think.

He doesn't.

"We're going to have a Fresh Air Fund kid come stay with us." Oscar must be remembering how hard we worked at our school to collect money for that charity.

"Dummy," I inform him. "They send needy kids from the city to the country. They are not going to send a kid *from* New York City to stay with a family *in* New York City."

"Stop calling your brother names," the rabbit says.

"Dummy is only one name, not names." I put the fork in my salad, spear some lettuce, and stick it into the rabbit's mouth.

My father catches the food in the napkin and puts the rabbit by the side of the plate.

Feeding the rabbit gets rid of it every time.

"Actually, Oscar is on the right track," my father informs us.

"So I'm not such a dummy after all." Oscar sticks his tongue out at me.

"Someday your tongue is going to get frozen like that," I tell him. "It happened to someone in my class. He stuck his tongue out in the third grade and now, every year, at Christmas, we string some tinsel and put a few ornaments on it."

"That's not true." Oscar looks at my parents. "Is it?"

For a genius, he is so gullible.

"No." My mother tries not to laugh. "Kendra Kaye, stop teasing your brother."

"So what's the surprise?" Oscar is known for his persistence.

"He's not a Fresh Air Fund kid." My father laughs at his own words. "We're going to have a farm kid come to the City for the summer. He's sort of an Un-Fresh Air Fund Kid."

"What?" I put down my fork. *Him?* A boy? How old? Where is he from? How do we know him? Why are we doing this? Where are we going to put him?"

"Is he my age?" Oscar asks. "Does he have his own television? Does he get just five hours of watching time too? Can he stay in my room?"

"He's not going to stay in mine," I inform everyone.

"Slow down, kids," my mother says. "We'll explain everything. Just be calm."

Calm. They're bringing another boy into our house —one probably just as repulsive as Oscar. Just what I need—two brats to take care of.

"Remember how we've mentioned our friends, the Lees, the couple we met at the Murder-on-the-Slopes weekend before you two were born? You know, where we went skiing and solved a make-believe murder, staged especially for the group?" my mother reminds us. "Anyway, they own a farm in Wisconsin and have the opportunity to live in Europe for the summer, and they want their son to stay with us and experience New York City life."

"Why not European life?" I think about all of my friends who've been lucky enough to go there.

"There are personal reasons." My father uses the tone of voice that means no more discussion about it.

"What's his name? How old is he?" Oscar raises his hand as if he's still in school.

He hasn't gotten used to summer vacation yet.

His method works though.

He gets answers.

"His name is Franklin—Frank, for short—and he's fifteen years old," my mother tells us.

My age. Or close, anyway.

"Don't you remember?" she continues. "We get a lovely Christmas card from the Lees each year with a picture and a very nice note."

I don't remember, but Oscar does.

He says, "Didn't they send a picture last year of the father, the mother, the boy, and their pet cow, Rover?"

"How do you remember stuff like that?" I ask.

"Easy. How many cards do we get each year like that? They are the only people that I've ever heard of with a pet cow named Rover."

"That's probably because we don't live in the suburbs. I've heard that everyone who doesn't live in a city has a pet cow. Not all are named Rover. Some are called Spot. And some also have sheep named Tabby," my father tells us.

Sometimes I think that my father has a case of acute silliness. I told him that once and he said that what he has is a *cute* silliness.

He continues, "He won't be bringing Rover to the City."

"If he did bring Rover to the City and the cow wasn't house-trained, we'd have to name the carpet Spot," I say.

Sometimes I think that terminal silliness is hereditary.

It hits me. They're bringing a boy my own age into the apartment to live all summer. And they wouldn't even let Jeremy and me be alone in the apartment.

Parents. They're not always easy to figure out.

What if this guy and I don't really get along? Or what if we start to really get along well? Or become "romantically involved" and he's living here? What are they going to do about our being alone together in the same apartment? Will they make one of us wait outside on some park bench until they get home from work? What if I think Frank is really doofy? What if he thinks I'm really doofy? What if he doesn't fit into our lives? It's not like when they brought home a baby brother whom I could help mold. Although in Oscar's case, instead of being well molded, he turned out moldy.

"Why didn't you discuss this with us?" I ask.

"That's what we're doing now." My mother passes me some avocado slices, which I usually love, but I'm not in the mood for bribes.

"It's all decided. That's not a discussion. That's tyranny." I take an avocado. I may not be in the mood for bribes, but I'm definitely in the mood for avocados.

"I understand how you're feeling," my father says. "Trust us on this. If we did it this way, there's a good reason. Please understand."

I sit quietly, trying to take it all in.

"Give it a chance. Please, honey." My mother passes me the avocado plate again. "It'll be fine."

I think about it.

If it's that important to my parents, maybe I should give it a chance. Anyway, my long history of knowing my parents helps me to realize that arguing would be a lost cause.

"OK," I say.

"It's OK with O.K., too," Oscar informs us.

"Great," my mother says. "And when the Lees arrive here next week, we will have a *big* surprise for you."

"In addition to this one?" I take two avocado slices.

My father nods. "Trust us. It's a terrific surprise."

We'll just see about that, I think, as I push the food around on my plate and think again about the caterpillars.

Cocoon life may seem a little closed in, but at least they don't have to share their cocoon with strangers.

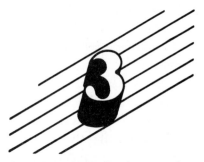

"Where's your sense of adventure?" Bethany asks, as we all change clothes at my pajama party. "Maybe this guy, Frank, will be the man of your dreams—smart, sexy, funny, cute, and sensitive. Maybe he'll walk into your house and it'll be love at first sight."

"Or maybe lust at first sight, which wouldn't be bad either." Bonnie puts on a black lace short nightgown.

"He could also be a real downer," I inform everyone as I quickly put on an extra-large purple nightshirt.

"You're so negative sometimes," Ama says, and Akosua agrees.

They're wearing matching pink nightgowns, covered by matching pink robes. The only difference in the twins' outfits is that Ama is wearing Garfield slippers and Akosua has on Odie slippers.

Personally, I hate slippers that look like cartoon characters and animals. It always seems like they look up under your nightshirt.

Teri comes out of the bathroom, where she has changed into her flowered nightgown. She's the only person I know who is shier than I am about showing off her body.

"That outfit is so gross," Bonnie says to Bethany.

Laughing, Bethany pretends to model her Smurfs pajamas. "I borrowed it from my sister in honor of tonight's pajama party. It's like old times."

"About Frank," Shannon says. "If it turns out that he's absolutely terrific, send him my way."

"You're going to be in Montana." Bethany takes out a container of magenta mousse and starts to design a new hairstyle for herself.

"Don't remind me." Shannon shakes her head. "Seeing my father means seeing my stepmother and her two gross kids. Oh, retch. Oh, well. It will give my mother the chance to be alone with her new husband—Number Five, I call him. It's such a pain to learn all of their names when she just divorces them eventually. It all makes me so sick. I just wish that I had my own apartment already, my own life."

"Don't we all? It would be so good if we could all get an apartment together," Teri says.

Bethany looks around. "It would probably be great for about two weeks and then we'd drive each other nuts."

"Or cause allergy attacks." I think about how neat I'd have to be if we all lived together. Friends don't think bad habits are so bad if they don't have to live with them.

"Oh, well. I guess we'll just have to go on the way we are," Shannon says. "It's off to Montana for me. Then back to New York when the summer's over."

"About Frank." Bethany returns to my problem. "If it turns out that he's absolutely terrific, maybe this will be your first big romance. Jeremy was a good start, but now it's time to meet someone new."

Easy for Bethany to say. She's always falling in love with some guy—and what's more, they always fall in love with her, too. She's so lucky.

"Frank could really turn out to be a doof," Bonnie says.

Or he could really think that *I'm* a doof, and then I'll be stuck with him thinking that all summer, I think but do not say out loud.

"If it's a nightmare, you can call me anytime or come visit me in the Hamptons to escape."

I think about Bethany's offer. It could be Great Fun or a Great Disaster. In the City, it's not so apparent that her family is ultrawealthy, although they live in their own building, a brownstone. The place in the country, however, has a zillion rooms, a swimming pool, and all of these movie-type people around, because her father is a big producer. I feel a little out of it when I go there—not sure of how to act, what to say. It's weird, I know, since Bethany's my best friend, but somehow it's hard. Last summer I went there and it took two days to get up enough nerve to be seen in my bathing suit. And then when I finally did, I got a terrible sunburn and couldn't wear anything else *but* my swimsuit for the next two days. Actually, I could also wear ointment, but that was about it.

"Bring sunscreen this time." Bonnie applies Lee's Press-On Nails to Teri's hands.

"Don't worry so much," Ama says. "You've spent the last two days absolutely obsessed about this guy and you haven't even met him."

"It's OK for Kendra to worry," Akosua says.

"You're just saying that because you worry about stuff too," Teri says, putting eyeliner on her.

"I'm not worried. I just think it's going to be a little weird that Ama and I won't be together, as twins. Even though it was our idea to go to different camps, it's still going to be strange."

"We've really been together since the beginning," Ama says.

I think about how weird it would be to have to share the same space since the very moment you become whatever you become when your parents do it and "it" becomes the beginning of a larger family.

Ama and Akosua not only share a *room* at their home—they also shared a *womb* once upon a time. I think about that. If they become weavers, they could also share a *loom* . . . they once were part of a baby *boom* . . . the only other rhyme I can think of is *tomb,* so I quit this line of thought.

"When I go to camp, I'm going to pretend that I'm an only child," Ama says.

"Me too," Akosua agrees. "No one else I know has the name, Ama, which means girl child born on Saturday or Akosua, a girl child born on Sunday."

"If we lived in South Ghana," Ama says. "I'm sure we'd know more people with our names, but we live on Central Park West."

They really are so close and so much alike that it'll

be very interesting to see what they'll be like at the end of summer.

"Do you think I should get my hair cut before I go away or should I get it done in Paris?" Teri looks up from a fashion magazine.

"Paris!" everyone yells.

"You're so lucky. Going to Paris to really learn the language," Shannon says.

"And to really learn how to French kiss," Bonnie teases.

Teri blushes. "That's not what I'm going for. You know that I want to major in French someday."

"Well, you can always be a minor in French kissing," Bonnie says.

Out of all of us, Bonnie's the one who's grown up the fastest. She looks the oldest and has parents who let her do whatever she wants to do. Actually, sometimes I think that they even let her do stuff that she's not sure that she wants to do, but who knows? She has false I.D. and goes to all the clubs and stays out later than the rest of us. Sometimes I wonder if she's even going to hang out with us much longer.

It's kind of weird when someone you've known practically forever changes so much so fast.

Oscar knocks on the door. "Can I come in?"

"No!" I yell.

Several of the girls yell, "Yes. Sure."

"No!" I yell again.

He comes in anyway. "The majority said yes."

Bethany smiles at him.

She actually likes the little creep. I think that they

got to be friends when he offered to help her with her science homework.

She got an A on her project. I got a C. I'd *never* ask the little whiz twerp for help.

He looks at me and smiles. "The pizza's here. I'm supposed to let you know. You're supposed to share it with me. Mom said so."

"We'll be out in a minute." I push him out the door. "Now scram."

He does.

"You shouldn't be so mean to him. He's kind of cute," Shannon says.

She only feels that way because she's an only child.

"Food," Bonnie says, putting on a robe. "Let's go. I'm starved."

Bonnie eats everything and never gains an ounce.

This summer she's going to be an apprentice in a summer stock theater and I bet she comes back as skinny and beautiful as ever.

As everyone else rushes into the dining room to get the pizza, I think about how they're all going away and I'll be the only one of the group left in the City.

Bethany said that it will probably be good for me.

We'll see about that.

One thing I know is that I don't want to think about it anymore.

The other thing I know is that I'd better get out there and eat before all of the sausage-with-extra-cheese pizza is gone.

"Just let him be frank with you." Bethany giggles over the phone.

"This is no time for puns," I tell her. "My family is meeting the Lees in less than an hour. It's easy for you to joke. Your parents haven't told you that you have to do something you don't want to do."

"My parents tell me that I have to do stuff that I don't want to do all the time," Bethany says. "All over the world, parents do that. Kendra, what's going on? Why are you being so weird?"

I play with the telephone cord while I think.

Bethany waits at the other end.

"I don't know. I really do feel weird," I say.

Bethany tells me, "Let's try to figure this out. Why are you so nervous about Frank coming to stay with your family?"

"I don't know him. He's a stranger." I really want to understand why I feel the way I do. "Does that seem strange?"

"So?" she says. "Lots of people would be excited by having a new person in the family. Is it Frank? Do you know something about him that makes you nervous? Would it be like this for anybody? Remember when the school played host to foreign students for a week? You and your family applied. It was fun."

"But that was only for a week. And anyway, we requested that a girl stay with us. It's going to be kind of weird to have a boy here—one who is not a father or brother."

I decided to tell her the thing that seems like a deep dark secret. "Bethany, I don't understand boys. I mean, I like a lot of them—I want to have one as a boyfriend. But I'm not always sure how to act around boys. Sometimes they act like they're from another planet."

There's silence for a minute, and then she laughs. "Kendra, I agree, boys aren't always easy to understand."

It's such a relief to hear her say that.

Now that I've started talking about it, the rest of my feelings pour out. "Oh, Bethany. I just don't understand. When we were in elementary school, it was so much easier. We were just little kids all playing together. And then there was the year that all of the boys ran around screaming 'Cooties' and pretending to pull bugs off of us and saying stuff like 'Barfola.' "

Bethany giggles and says, "And we all kept saying that they were so gross."

"And then it all started to change," I say.

"Yes."

"So now I just don't know anymore. What to say, what to do, what they're going to say, what they're going to do. And now I'm going to have some guy living in my house. I'm not going to have privacy. I'm always going to be a little on edge."

"I see your point," Bethany says.

We're both quiet for a few minutes.

"Maybe . . ." she starts.

"Please don't say 'Maybe you'll learn from this experience,' " I say.

There's quiet at both ends of the phone.

There's a knock at my door and my father calls in, "We're leaving now. We've got to meet the Lees at Tavern-on-the-Green."

"Gotta go," I tell Bethany.

"Good luck, pal," Bethany says.

"Thanks, pal," I tell her. "Listen—maybe I'll learn from this experience."

Grabbing my sunglasses, I walk into the living room.

My parents are all dressed up.

So is Oscar, who hates having to wear a tie.

I love it when he has to wear a tie.

My outfit consists of a black skirt, pink tunic blouse, silver link belt, and sandals. Also one dangling pink earring in my right earlobe and a black pearl in my left.

I wonder what the Lees will wear. Something off the farm, I bet. OshKosh B'Gosh ties and overalls for the guys, and a little pinafore for Mrs. Lee.

As we leave the apartment building and walk down the street, my father points across to Central Park. "Look at all the people going into the Park. I bet a lot of them are going to the Shakespeare Festival. Summer is such a great time to be in the City."

"So are the rest of the seasons," my mother says.

Sometimes they sound like a paid advertisement for the City.

My father puts his arm around my mother's shoulder and she puts her arm around his waist.

I wonder if my father ever ran around screaming "Cooties!" I wonder if Frank runs around screaming "Cooties!"

We walk along Central Park West.

So many people are on the street, walking, riding skateboards, riding bikes, in cars, carrying balloons, eating food.

Somewhere nearby there's got to be a street fair going on. On a summer weekend, there are always street fairs.

On one corner we pass a man who looks kind of familiar. He's walking with his family.

For two blocks I try to figure out who he was. A teacher? Someone's parent? Then I figure it out. He's an actor on some TV show. In New York City there are a lot of famous people on the street, because many of them live here.

As we continue to walk, my father says, "Now, here's the plan. We'll all have dinner together and you'll find out about the surprise. Then the grown-ups will go back to the apartment to discuss some things and the kids will go to a movie."

"Good!" Oscar jumps up and down. "Can we see something PG or R?"

"No."

"How come you want to get rid of us?" I want to know.

"Because we've got some planning to do," my father says. "We have to finalize our surprise. You kids will love what's happening. I promise you."

People should never make promises unless they're absolutely sure they're true.

My father continues, "Then tomorrow you kids will have some time to look over some special materials without the adults around. Then we'll take Mr. and Mrs. Lee to the airport. And then, on the next day, you can begin." He smiles. "This is going to be so much fun. Just you wait and see."

"You'll just have to be careful," my mother says.

"Janet, there's nothing to worry about," my father tells her. "This is so terrific. I only wish that something like this had happened to me when I was a kid."

She says nothing.

I'm getting very curious.

"Here we are, Tavern-on-the-Green," my father announces as we enter this building that looks like it has been built by elves for royalty.

I always feel like a character in a fairy tale when I come here—or maybe a little like Alice in Wonderland.

We go through a long hall with rooms on the left side. We get to the Crystal Room. You've got to request it when reservations are made. With glass all around and on the ceiling, it's like being in a greenhouse that grows wonderful sparkly things from the ceiling. The many-colored crystal chandeliers gleam like elephant earrings. The trees outside glitter with thousands of tiny white lights.

As we walk past the marble elks, I pat one and almost expect it to come to life.

Everything seems so magical.

It's so pretty that I almost forget what we're here for.

It's not really possible to forget, though. At the table, waiting for us, are the Lees.

Be still, my heart.

That's what my Aunt Judy, who moved to England, always says when she sees some really attractive actor in the movies or on television.

Be still, my heart.

That's what I say to myself when I see Frank Lee.

First I notice that he's tall—about six feet, blond hair, and the kind of body that looks like it exercises or lifts cows or hay or something.

When we all sit down at the table, I look at Frank's face. I'm glad I'm wearing sunglasses so no one can tell that I'm staring.

He has really nice features. He's so cute. It makes me very nervous.

"Kendra, honey, you forgot to take off your sunglasses." My mother touches my arm.

Drats.

Removing my sunglasses, I can really see his face.

However, now he can see my face too and know I'm staring at him.

I look down at the plate. My heartbeat, I'm sure,

can be heard all the way to New Jersey. Bethany's probably hearing it in the Hamptons.

Frank has sky-blue eyes, framed by thick brown eyelashes.

Looking at me, he nods and says, "Hello."

I feel as if he can immediately tell that I'm a little shy around B-O-Y-S.

"I'm Oscar Kaye. That means I'm O.K. and you're not." Oscar reaches over to shake Frank's hand and knocks over a water glass.

Water spills all over the table and onto my lap.

I jump up.

Everyone can see that my skirt is soaking wet.

It looks like I need Pampers.

I could die of embarrassment.

I could kill Oscar, who at this moment is definitely not OK in my book. Why does he have to pick this time to be a perfect gentleman?

The waiter brings over a dry chair and a lot of extra napkins.

Everyone in the place is probably staring at us.

I feel like Alice in Waterland.

Sitting down, I say, "Let's pretend that nothing's happened and just go on with the conversation."

Everyone smiles and finally introductions are made.

The Lees are not wearing overalls.

In fact, they are dressed, as my Aunt Judy would say, "very spiffy."

Mrs. Lee's got on a basic black dress with a single strand of pearls and Mr. Lee looks like a businessman in a three-piece suit.

Frank's got on a pair of gray pants and a shirt almost the same color as his sky-blue eyes.

They are not chewing on pieces of hay.

All of the parents are saying things like, "Remember how all of this started? How we met? How much has happened since then!"

I sneak a look at Frank, who looks no more excited by their conversation than I feel.

He looks in my direction.

I stare up at the part of the ceiling where it comes down a little and it is painted with birds and flowers. With the way that it's positioned above the tables, it looks like the birds could drop something on the tables.

Then I look outside into the open garden, where there is a real possibility that a pigeon could do that.

Oscar is very quiet, keeping his hands off the table and away from glasses. Leaning over, he whispers, "Kendra, I'm sorry."

"You should be," I whisper back, smiling as if nothing's the matter but wondering whether the very large chandeliers have ever fallen on clumsy younger brothers.

The waiter takes the drink orders.

Because I've had enough water for the day, I say, "Pepsi, please."

My clothes are still wet, although my body has dried off.

Frank has said very little except for the initial hello.

I haven't said much either. "Pepsi, please" is not exactly brilliant conversation.

The waiter brings our drinks and takes our meal orders.

Oscar orders his regular, cheeseburger with bacon.

I order trout.

The adults all order steak.

So does Frank.

"Don't you feel weird, living on a farm, having a pet cow, and eating steak?" I ask.

"Kendra," my mother says.

"We raise beef to sell. It's business," Mr. Lee says.

"Rover's a pet. We don't eat our pets," Frank says.

"Are you a vegetarian?" Mrs. Lee asks.

"No. I just don't eat certain things, like venison, because that would be like eating Bambi, the deer in the cartoon."

"You eat tuna fish sandwiches," Oscar says. "That's like eating Charlie the Tuna in the commercials."

"Oh, Oscar. It's not the same." I shake my head.

"When I was in the seventh grade, I used to have a girlfriend who was a vegetarian. We disagreed about this all the time." Frank cuts a piece of his steak.

Is she still your girlfriend? I want to ask, but don't.

Frank turns to his parents. "You didn't like her either. Remember?"

The Lees say nothing.

"So what grade are you in?" Mr. Lee turns to me.

"Going into tenth," I reply.

"Frank too." Mr. Lee looks very thin and a little tired.

Frank stares down at his silverware, looking like he's going to explode before he ever sees tenth grade.

I almost wish that Oscar would spill another glass of water on someone—even me—to distract things.

Luckily, the waiter arrives with our food. The adults change the subject, talking to each other about Europe.

They're so lucky. I've always wanted to go to Europe—especially England, since I can already speak the language.

I look over at Frank, who still looks as if he's going to explode.

I'm going to have to spend six weeks with this person?

Day camp might have been easier.

He looks over at me and sort of half smiles.

"Look," he says softly, "this has nothing to do with you or your family. I'm sorry you're getting caught in the middle of this."

I wonder what "this" is.

I look over at my parents to see if they know what's going on and I try to figure out if they're upset.

They don't seem to be.

The adults just keep talking, and keep talking, and keep talking. . . .

Finally, dessert arrives.

Cheesecake with strawberries. Heaven. Not a second too soon.

Everyone finally seems calm.

"So what's the surprise?" O.K. is practically jumping out of his chair.

My parents smile at the Lees.

"I guess this is as good a time as any to explain the

plan. Why don't you tell them, Ernie." Mr. Lee nods to my father.

My father is grinning. "As you know, Frank will be staying with us for a large part of the summer."

I look at Frank, who looks much calmer.

My father continues. "As you know, we don't want you kids to hang around all summer being couch potatoes, just watching television. So, we've worked out a terrific, truly wonderful, fantastic plan."

Whenever my father gets excited, he uses a lot of adjectives.

I hope that this is good.

"So," he continues, "since we live in one of the greatest cities in the world—one which we want Kendra and O.K. to really know—we've devised a very special scavenger hunt. Actually, more than a scavenger hunt. For facts, for souvenirs, for reports, and most of all, for fun."

"Is this like a class trip?" O.K. asks.

"In a way, but much more fun. Thirty-five days will be well spent exploring the City," my father says. "It'll be phenomenal, wonderful, fantastic!"

"You just have to promise to be very careful, roaming the city." My mother stirs her coffee.

"We've set up a special fund for you to be able to pay for everything," Mrs. Lee says.

"And a special reward when you do everything on the list," my father says.

"What? What?" O.K. is so excited.

Call anything a reward and he's happy.

When he was much younger, I used to be able to say

things like "O.K., if you clear the table, I'll give you a reward and let you help me wash the dishes."

That doesn't work anymore, but he still tends to be very optimistic about things.

"Complete the list and the reward will be . . ." My father pauses. He loves drama. "A trip to England for all of you, for all of us!"

England. I can't believe it.

"Not right after the six weeks in New York." Frank looks at his parents.

"Not right after the six weeks in New York," his mother says with a sigh.

O.K. jumps up and down.

"You must fulfill the requirements," Mr. Lee says.

"My father means that," Frank says. "Once he says something, that's it."

"Frank." His mother looks over at him.

I don't think this is all just about the trip to England.

Mr. Lee says, "That's true. The requirements must be fulfilled correctly, within the time limit."

My parents agree.

I think about it.

A scavenger hunt in New York City.

A trip to England as the prize.

There are some things that I'm not sure of, and while Frank and his family are some of those things, there is one thing that I'm sure of.

This summer is definitely getting more interesting.

SCAVENGER HUNT
MEMO
To: KENDRA, FRANK, AND O.K.
From: THEIR LOVING PARENTS

"Aarg," O.K. says as we sit in the kitchen and start reading the instructions. "I think they've lost their marbles."

"That's probably where they are right now, buying new ones. And I think that Dad's gone into overdrive using his new computer." I giggle.

"Loving parents," Frank says. "I wonder how long it took for them to decide to decide on that group name."

We look at the printout again.

Re: THE LeeKaye SCAVENGER HUNT

"With a name like that, it sounds like we'll have to scavenge in a boat with holes," O.K. says.

"They could have called it the KayeLee Scavenger

Hunt." I laugh. "That would make it sound like a search for cosmetics."

"Ring Ding?" O.K. offers everyone his favorite snack, which he has just taken out of the freezer section of our refrigerator.

"Sure." Frank smiles.

He smiles more often when his parents aren't around.

"Me too." I take one and start reading aloud.

" 'Rules and Regulations.' "

"Somehow I knew that would be part of any plan that my parents were involved with." Frank takes a large bite out of the Ring Ding.

It's weird sitting in my kitchen with this guy who I really don't know, but who I'll be spending a month and a half of my life with. Continuing to read, I say, " 'We, the loving parents, in order to form a more perfect union, do hereby devise an absolutely wonderful, marvelous educational experience in which our children search for objects, facts, people, and places.' "

I look up. "All those adjectives. I bet that Dad's responsible for that sentence."

"Read on." O.K. is already on his second Ring Ding.

No wonder his classmates call him The Bottomless Pit. If he eats like that, when he becomes a teenager I bet they'll refer to him as The Bottomless Zit.

I read on.

" 'To that end, we feel that there are certain rules that are self-evident. One. For the purposes of this Scavenger Hunt, the three individuals involved—Kendra, Frank, and O.K.—will be referred to as The Serendipities.' "

"I'll go get the dictionary and look up that word."
O.K. stands up.

"You don't have to," Frank says. *"Serendipity* is a word that my father uses a lot. It comes from some Persian fairy tale. It means the ability to make fortunate discoveries accidentally."

"Like if we fell in a hole and discovered gold."
O.K.'s committing the definition to his dictionary-like brain. "Or if we fell into a pile of you know what and discovered unicorns."

"Do you have to be so disgusting?" I make a face at him.

"Yes." He smiles at me.

Serendipity for me would be to have a family tree assignment and to discover that my parents had only borrowed O.K. and were planning to return him shortly.

He's the only person I know who discusses unicorn you-know-what.

I continue. " 'Two. The Serendipities are to be involved in this scavenger hunt together. There will be no splitting up. All three people go to every one of the places. Each to All is the general rule. The only acceptable excuse is if you are run over by a senior citizen riding a Harley-Davidson motorcycle.

" 'Three. No person is responsible for being the fact mavin, the individual who looks up all of the information. That job must be shared equally, to be called Teach for All.' "

"I wonder if our meal rules will be called 'Peach for All.' " Frank shakes his head.

"And if when we go to soak up some rays, then it'll be 'Beach for All.' " I get into the word game, even though I don't feel really comfortable with Frank yet.

"If we try to mooch off people, then that would be 'Leech for All.' " Frank starts laughing.

"If someone begs to be included in this hunt, then that would be 'Beseech Us All,' " I contribute.

"If we take the equipment at an athletic event, that would be 'Reach for Ball,' " Frank says.

"That was very dumb," O.K. tells him.

Frank throws a Ring Ding at him.

No complaints from O.K.

Frank really confuses me.

Sometimes he seems so angry.

Sometimes he's funny, so nice.

There are some really good reasons why I get confused about him.

He is not always the same, the way he acts.

Right now, though, I like what he's doing.

Silliness with words is one of my favorite things.

"And if we get lectured for doing something wrong, it would be 'Preach for All,' " Frank continues.

"Enough!" yells O.K. "What's next?"

I go back to the rules and regulations.

" 'Four. All requirements must be fulfilled within the time limit. It is up to the group to decide how to plan the time and visits and to proceed carefully.

" 'Five. Everyone must get along. There will be no

taking sides, no excluding one another, no name-calling.' "

"Yuck." O.K. looks at me. "That's going to be hard."

That, at least, is something we both agree on.

I go on.

" 'Six. Since there is a limited amount of time, the Scavenger Hunt will be confined to Manhattan.' "

"Isn't Manhattan New York City?" Frank asks.

"It's only one part of the city," O.K. explains.

"I have a lot to learn," Frank says. "It's so different here. Back home you can hear the crickets chirp."

"And the cows moo." O.K. giggles.

Frank nods. "Sometimes at night it's absolutely quiet."

O.K. starts to sing. " 'Oh, give me a home where the buffalo roam.' "

Frank throws another Ring Ding at him.

If Ring Ding Discus ever becomes an Olympic event, I expect to see Frank with a gold medal around his neck.

Frank continues. "Here it's so noisy. There are sirens screeching all the time, horns blaring, people playing radios loudly, all listening to different stations, conga drums—how can you get to sleep at night? And it's not just the noise. New York City is like a giant night-light with sound effects."

I laugh. "When I visit Bethany in the country, I get very nervous at night. It's just too quiet. Look," I say. "Enough talk about what a *loud* place this is. I should be *allowed* to continue reading."

Ducking as the Ring Ding flies over my head, I continue to read.

" 'Seven. The Serendipities are to keep an accurate day-by-day log to show that all of the requirements in the contract are met. At the end of each entry, each Serendipity will enter a comment about the day.

" 'This log, as well as the required information, will be recorded on the computer. At the end of the Scavenger Hunt, each Serendipity, as well as his or her parents, will receive a copy of the log as a memento.'

"Now for the Hunt," I say, and start to read again.

" 'Part One. The Facts Hunt. Question One. How many blocks are there in a Manhattan mile if you are going uptown or downtown (north–south)?' "

"I know that." O.K. claps his hands. "There are twenty blocks to a mile, eighteen sixty-foot-wide streets, two one-hundred-foot-wide streets, and twenty two-hundred-foot-long blocks."

"Is he always like this?" Frank smiles at Oscar.

"Yup," I say. "The family genius. 'Two. Why was "The Dakota" apartment building given its name? Give three other facts about the building.' "

O.K. jumps up again.

"Let's go through the questions first and then we'll do the answers," I suggest.

O.K. sits down.

" 'Three. What is New York City's nickname? Four. How long is Manhattan?' "

"Thirteen and four-tenths miles!" O.K. calls out.

" 'Five. How wide is Manhattan at its widest point?' "

"Two and three-tenths miles," O.K. informs us.

" 'Six. Where is the widest part of Manhattan Island?' "

Frank and I look at O.K., who says, "From river to river at about Eighty-seventh Street."

" 'Seven. How many boroughs are there in New York City?' "

O.K. counts on his fingers. "Five. Manhattan, the Bronx, Brooklyn, Queens, and Staten Island."

" 'Eight. Which of the five boroughs is the only one connected to the American mainland?' The Bronx," I say, very glad that I answered one before O.K.

" 'Nine. What about the rest of the boroughs?' All of the others are islands or part of Long Island," I say. "Listen. Let's just look at all the questions and answer them later.

" 'Ten. In which direction do avenues run?

" 'Eleven. In which direction do streets run?

" 'Twelve. When was New York City discovered?

" 'Thirteen. When distances from New York City are given, what Manhattan location is used?' "

"Columbus Circle!" O.K. yells out.

He's always had a problem with self-discipline.

" 'Fourteen. On what street will you find the narrowest house? After visiting it, give three facts about it, including its width.

" 'Fifteen. What is the name of the award given to Broadway plays and how did it get that name?

" 'Sixteen. What is the name of the award given to Off-Broadway plays and how did it get that name?

" 'Seventeen. What are the names of the two lions in

front of the main branch of the New York Public Library and who gave them these names?

" 'Eighteen. What does SoHo mean? NoHo?

" 'Nineteen. What does TriBeCa mean?

" 'Twenty. How many acres is Central Park and what are its boundaries?

" 'Twenty-One. Name fifteen important facts that you learn when visiting the Park *(DURING DAYTIME HOURS).*

" 'Twenty-Two. Draw a map showing all of the sections of Manhattan.'

"This is a lot of work," I say. "I live here and I don't know a lot of the answers."

"I don't either," O.K. says.

I love to hear that.

"I certainly don't. This place is definitely not like my hometown," Frank tells us. "When I was really little the only things that I knew about New York came from the old songs that my parents liked to listen to, like 'New York, New York' and 'Give My Regards to Broadway.' "

O.K. starts to hum the second song and tap-dance like in the movie.

Frank laughs. "I never got that song right. I thought that the words were 'Remember me to Harold Square,' like Harold was some big-shot like the mayor or something."

I giggle. "It's *Herald* Square—what they call the area near Macy's."

"Now I know." Frank grins.

O.K. starts the song and we all join in.

" 'Give my regards to Broadway,
   Remember me to Harold Square.
   Tell all the gang at Forty-Second Street that
   I will soon be there.
   Whisper of how I'm yearning
   To mingle with the old time throng.
   Give my regards to old Broadway
   and say that I'll be there ere long.' "

We all look at each other and laugh.

Something tells me that the Scavenger Hunt may turn out to be a lot of fun.

Frank picks up another Ring Ding and acts like he's holding a Frisbee.

"To me." O.K. raises his hands.

Frank tosses the Ring Ding to O.K., who immediately puts it in his mouth, forgetting that it's still wrapped in foil.

"How much more is there of the fact section?" Frank wants to know.

"Don't ask." That's what I always say when something is too much.

"Let's hear more." O.K. has crumbs all over his shirt.

" 'Twenty-three. What does *Manhattan* mean?

" 'Twenty-four. Was New York ever the nation's capital?' "

O.K. nods yes.

" 'Twenty-Five. In 1626, how much did Peter Minuit pay for Manhattan and what is the most interesting fact about the transaction?' "

"I know that already!" O.K. jumps up and down. "Minuit gave a group of Indians sixty guilders worth twenty-four dollars—and this is the best part—the Indians that he bought it from were not from Manhattan at all. My teacher said that even though it's not a positive fact, he thinks that the land had to be bought again later."

Frank, O.K., and I look at each other and start to laugh.

The more I think about the island being sold by people who didn't own it, the funnier it gets.

Obviously we all think that it's very humorous, because we can't stop laughing.

As soon as we stop, one of us starts laughing again and then the rest of us start laughing.

"They didn't own it." Frank puts his head down on the table.

"And Minuit bought it." O.K. drops a Ring Ding on the floor and accidentally steps on it.

Finally we calm down.

Let's go on to the next section," Frank says.

"All right," I continue.

" 'Part Two. The Places.

" 'Choose twenty (include the fourteen starred museums). Visit and bring back the admission buttons or one souvenir and list one fact about it.

" 'Note: It is not enough to just get the proof of entry. The Serendipities are to really explore the museums.' "

Looking at Frank, I say, "My parents are always

making games out of things to try to make life more interesting. Are your parents like that too?"

"Let's not talk about my parents right now, please." He makes a really gross face.

"Will you ever tell us what's going on?" I'm surprised by my boldness.

He nods. "One of these days. Today let's just look at the list."

I pick up the papers again and show everyone the Column A list.

COLUMN A
THE MUSEUMS
(Go to 20 including the 14 starred)

★ AMERICAN CRAFT MUSEUM
★ AMERICAN MUSEUM OF NATURAL HISTORY
  HAYDEN PLANETARIUM
  AMERICAN NUMISMATIC SOCIETY
  ASIA SOCIETY
  CHINA HOUSE GALLERY
★ THE CLOISTERS
  COOPER–HEWITT MUSEUM
  THE FRICK COLLECTION
★ THE SOLOMON R. GUGGENHEIM MUSEUM
  HISPANIC SOCIETY
★ INTERNATIONAL CENTER OF PHOTOGRAPHY
  JAPAN HOUSE GALLERY
★ JEWISH MUSEUM
  LIBRARY AND MUSEUM OF THE
    PERFORMING ARTS

★ METROPOLITAN MUSEUM OF ART
PIERPONT MORGAN LIBRARY
MUSEUM OF AMERICAN FOLK ART
MUSEUM OF THE AMERICAN INDIAN
MUSEUM OF THE CITY OF NEW YORK
★ MUSEUM OF MODERN ART
NATIONAL ACADEMY OF DESIGN
★ NEW-YORK HISTORICAL SOCIETY
★ NEW YORK PUBLIC LIBRARY
SOUTH STREET SEAPORT MUSEUM
STUDIO MUSEUM IN HARLEM
★ WHITNEY MUSEUM OF AMERICAN ART
ABIGAIL ADAMS SMITH MUSEUM
AFRICAN-AMERICAN INSTITUTE
ALTERNATIVE MUSEUM
★ AMERICAN MUSEUM OF IMMIGRATION
FASHION INSTITUTE OF TECHNOLOGY
INTREPID SEA-AIR-SPACE MUSEUM
EL MUSEO DEL BARRIO
★ MUSEUM OF BROADCASTING
★ MUSEUM OF HOLOGRAPHY
THEATRE MUSEUM
FIRE DEPARTMENT MUSEUM
SCHOMBURG CENTER FOR RESEARCH IN
BLACK CULTURE

"The number of museums in New York City is amazing," Frank says.

"That's just Manhattan," I remind him.

COLUMN B
THE PLACES
(Choose 15, including the 7 starred choices)

CITY HALL
CHRYSLER BUILDING
* RADIO CITY MUSIC HALL
* WORLD TRADE CENTER
CUSTOM HOUSE
GENERAL GRANT NATIONAL MEMORIAL
FULTON FISH MARKET
GUINNESS WORLD RECORDS EXHIBIT AT
    THE EMPIRE STATE BUILDING
NEW YORK HORTICULTURAL SOCIETY
RIVERSIDE CHURCH
ST. PATRICK'S CATHEDRAL
* ROCKEFELLER CENTER
ROOSEVELT ISLAND AND TRAMWAY
SOLDIERS AND SAILORS MONUMENT
* STATUE OF LIBERTY
* UNITED NATIONS
* ELLIS ISLAND
CASTLE CLINTON
CATHEDRAL CHURCH OF ST. JOHN THE
    DIVINE
CONGREGATION SHEARITH ISRAEL
* LINCOLN CENTER
CARNEGIE HALL
THEODORE ROOSEVELT BIRTHPLACE

COLUMN C
THE AREAS
(Visit fifteen of the following areas, including the 7 starred ones. Note: A Parent will accompany you to some of these areas. Check first.)

LOWER EAST SIDE
* CHINATOWN
* LITTLE ITALY
* SoHo
* TRIBECA
  EAST VILLAGE
  GREENWICH VILLAGE
  CHELSEA
  MURRAY HILL
  GRAMERCY PARK
  GARMENT DISTRICT
* THEATRE DISTRICT
  MIDTOWN
  TUDOR CITY
  UPPER EAST SIDE
  YORKVILLE
* LINCOLN CENTER AREA
  UPPER WEST SIDE
  (Since you live here, do not include this one.)
  MORNINGSIDE HEIGHTS
  HARLEM
  EAST HARLEM
* CENTRAL PARK
  STUYVESANT
  BOWERY

WALL ST.
WHITE HALL
LOWER WEST SIDE

COLUMN D
TO DO
(Choose 8)

SEE A BROADWAY PLAY
SEE THE ROCKETTES
GO TO A BALLET
GET THE SIGNATURES OF 20 FOREIGN
    VISITORS (Carefully)
SEE A TV SHOW BEING FILMED
GO TO A CONCERT
SEE SHAKESPEARE IN THE PARK
VISIT STRAWBERRY FIELDS
GO BACKSTAGE ON BROADWAY
GO TO AN OPERA

Frank clutches at his throat and pretends to go into a faint. "Not an opera—please, not an opera! Anything but an opera."

O.K. falls to the ground, smushing the Ring Ding that he had previously dropped. "Death before opera."

They spend the next three minutes in various stages of agony.

I look at the two people with whom I will be spending most of the summer and wonder what I'm letting myself in for.

"Look, guys," I say. "I don't want to go to the opera

either. I bet that Mom is the one who put it on the list. She's never gotten over the time, three years ago, that she took us both to the opera and we got terrible stomachaches that immediately got better as soon as we left."

"It also didn't help that I made a loud burp during that really serious romantic part," O.K. informs us. "No opera. It's agreed. Now how much more do they have planned for us?"

We look down at the paper.

COLUMN E
(The Serendipities are to widen their food horizons this summer.)

"I guess that means I can eat more Ring Dings." O.K. grins.

"Horizons aren't the only thing that will widen." I look at his rear end.

"You're not funny." He makes a face at me. "If they hadn't said no name calling, you can imagine what some of the names would be."

"Moments like this, I'm glad that I'm an only child," Frank states.

There are times when Frank sounds much older than he is, than the boys in my class. Maybe it's because he's an only child. Maybe it's because he actually is a year older. I just made the cut-off date for admission to school and so I'm one of the youngest in my class and he just missed his cut-off date, so he's older.

"Let's see what they have planned for us now,"
Frank says.

We look at the sheet.

You are to try everything on this list at least once.
And we don't want any complaining.

"There better not be sushi—raw fish—on this list,"
Frank says. "The only way I like sushi is cooked."

"Then it's not sushi," O.K. says.

"Exactly." Frank nods.

We go back to the list.

> Pasta
> Kosher deli sandwich
> Chinese food (the different kinds)
> Mexican food
> Indian food (American)
> Indian food
> Sushi

"Yuga." Frank goes into his choking routine.

> Fondue
> Food from street vendors
> Afghani
> Pizza
> Knishes
> Chitlins and other soul food
> Bagels, cream cheese, and lox
> French food

Jambalaya
Meal cooked by Serendipities

"Oh no," we all say at once.

Yorkshire pudding
Hamburgers

"Thank goodness," Frank says.

Thai
Vietnamese
Cuban

"Is this stuff going to be hard to find?" Frank asks.

"No. New York is a gastronomic wonderland." O.K. sounds like one of those "I Love New York" television commercials.

"Is gas the operative word?" Frank makes a face. "Is most of this stuff edible?"

"I hope so." I cross my fingers. "I've had some of it —not all, though."

"I live on a farm in a small town that has about four restaurants. One's a combination pizza–Laundromat, another's a McDonald's. Then there's a Chinese restaurant. It's owned and run by the McGuire family. The food is terrible. And then there's the one good American-style restaurant."

"Pizza–Laundromat?" O.K. goes for another Ring Ding. "That sounds terrific."

I watch him snurfle down another fattening thing

take the Serendipities to England if all of the requirements are fulfilled.

They've already signed it.
We look at each other.
"What do you think?" I ask.
"If we don't do this," O.K. looks at me and says, "our parents will be very unhappy."
"So?" Frank makes a face.
I stare at him. "Forget that reason for a minute. Think about this instead. We have to fill up six weeks' worth of time. You know how much that is. This sounds like fun—most of it anyway."
He thinks for a minute and then says, "Actually, it does. And being with the two of you is the first good time I've had for a while."
I like that he said that. He really didn't have to include O.K. though.
"Also, don't forget about England," I say. "My Aunt Judy is really terrific. You'll like her. And it'll be fun to go. So let's do it."
"I want to." O.K. gets up and signs the paper.
Frank and I look at each other and smile.
We sign.
It's official.
The Serendipities—get ready for New York.
New York—get ready for The Serendipities.
By the time we win, even good old "Harold Square" will remember us.

and wonder how come he never gains weight. should be a rolling butterball, the way that he eats.

"This will be fun," I say, not really positive myse

"We'll see." Frank looks very doubtful. "I'm n sure about all of this weird food. I'm going to keep secret stash of peanut butter and jelly in my room."

"You have to be careful of roaches, living in New York." This time O.K. does not sound like a television commercial. "All of the neighborhoods have them."

Gross. Does he have to mention roaches?

My mother is a clean-aholic, so we hardly ever have a problem.

"I'll keep it clean. I just have to know that there is real food to be eaten during the summer."

"We won't have to eat the other stuff all the time. We just have to try it." O.K. is very sure of himself. "I know our parents are just trying to get us to 'broaden our horizons,' as they're always saying."

I look down at the paper. "That's it. All we have to do now is make it official."

The guys come over and look at the last page.

THE CONTRACT

We, The Serendipities, do hereby promise to meet all of the requirements—to do all the things, to go to all of the places, and to find out all of the facts.

signed

KENDRA KAYE
OSCAR KAYE
FRANKLIN LEE

We, the Loving Parents, do hereby promise to

Dear Kendra,
Paris is
beautiful! But
I'm so homesick
I could die!
Wish you were
here. Write
immediately.
xxxxx Jeri

Kendra Kaye
1592 W. 86th St
Apt 10D
NY, NY
10024

Dear Kendra,
It's sooo boring here!
The step bro & sis are
PAINS!!!

I wish I were there!
!!!!!!!!!!!!!!!!!!!!!!!!
♡ Shannon

Dear Kendra,
Camp Adirondack
is fun. The kids are
nice. I miss my sister.
I miss the group.
Write soon.
Bye. Have to go
swimming now.
          Love, Ama

Dear Kendra,
Camp Catskill is fun.
The kids are nice.
I miss my sister.
I miss the group.
Write soon.
Bye. Have to go
swimming now. Love,
          Akosua

To: KENDRA
From: BETHANY
Re: A MAJOR PROBLEM

Yesterday, my father's new production got a TERRIBLE review in "The N.Y. Times."

Yesterday, the phone bill arrived. We're still wiping my father off the ceiling.

TODAY, my long distance phone calls have been limited to two a week..... and they can't be our normal hour long talks.

We're going to have to start writing to each other. What a nightmare!

Life can be so tragic sometimes.

It's a shame that "The N.Y. Times" doesn't publish parent reviews by kids.

Frantically yours,
Bethany

Reading each letter twice, I really miss the group.

I wonder how Bonnie is doing. Something tells me that she's not going to be much of a letter writer.

O.K. comes into the kitchen. "You know the letter that Frank just got—the one that stinks of perfume?"

I nod, very curious, but try to act as if I'm not. "What about it?"

"Well, he's in the bedroom and asked to be left alone while he reads it."

"Oh," I say.

O.K. continues. "I asked him what the big S.W.A.K. means. That's when he asked for privacy."

"Was he mean when he said it?" This is the seventh day of the Scavenger Hunt and I still don't have Frank figured out.

That shouldn't surprise me because I already know that I'm not at my best when it comes to figuring out what goes on in boys' minds.

"Not mean." O.K. takes a cold piece of pizza out of the refrigerator. "Just like he wanted to be alone. So what does S.W.A.K. mean? She Was A Kangaroo? Stuck With A Kendra?"

"Sealed With A Kiss, you little twerp," I explain.

"Ohhhhh." He makes the two letters sound like a very long word. "I bet that Frank's got a girlfriend."

"One who uses cheap perfume," I add.

"Kendra's jealous!" O.K. sings.

"Shut up and go away. I want to answer these letters," I tell him. "Leave me alone."

"I can't even stay in my own bedroom. Look, we're

done for the day. I'm going upstairs to play with Ralph."

He leaves and I think of how lucky he is to have someone his own age in the building.

There are twenty floors in the building and at least ten apartments on each floor. You'd think that there would be someone else my age in the building, but there isn't—wasn't before Frank moved in.

I start answering the letters that I've just gotten. It's a proven fact that if you don't write back to people, they won't write to you again.

Writing the first letter, I realize that it will take forever to tell each friend all of the stuff that the Serendipities have done for the past seven days.

Then it comes to me. All I have to do is send each of them a copy of the computer printout of the log that we have been keeping.

I rush to the printer, run off six copies, and reread one of them.

We really have done so much.

SERENDIPITY LOG

DAY 1

Parents (the Kayes, heretofore referred to as "The Ks") drive Serendipities all over the city on Sunday. Special stops on Lower East Side: Chinatown. Ate knishes at Yonah Shimmel. Ate salami, pastrami, corned beef sandwiches at Katz's.
THIS CITY IS AMAZING. Frank Lee (FL)

CAN I HELP IT IF I GET CAR SICK? Oscar Kaye (OK)
WHY DO I ALWAYS HAVE TO SIT NEXT TO O.K. IN CARS? IT'S NOT FAIR. Kendra Kaye (KK)

DAY 2

New York Public Library—to get facts. Guinness World Records Exhibit Hall in the Empire State Building. Hamburgers at the Automat.
THE MAIN BRANCH OF THE NEW YORK PUBLIC LIBRARY IS ABSOLUTELY AWESOME, NO LIES, TWO LIONS. (KK)
THE TALLEST MAN WHO EVER LIVED WAS ROBERT WADLOW. AT 8 FEET, 11.1 INCHES, MY SCHOOL BASKETBALL TEAM COULD HAVE REALLY USED HIM. (FL)
CAN I HELP IT IF HEIGHTS MAKE ME SICK? (OK)

DAY 3

Museums. Note: On Tuesday Nights they are free. Museum of Modern Art. American Craft Museum. We ate food sold by street vendors, and then for dinner we ate Indian food—the kind with curry.
I LOVED THE MUSEUMS. (KK)
I LOVED LUNCH. (OK)
I CAN'T BELIEVE HOW MANY DIFFERENT KINDS OF FOOD ARE SOLD ON THE STREET. THIS IS WHAT THEY MUST MEAN BY "A LA CART." (FL)

DAY 4

Museum of Holography. St. Patrick's Cathedral. TKTS (Broadway at 47th Street), where you can buy tickets to a lot of shows for half price, but you have to stand in a long line. We got tickets to *A Chorus Line.* Pizza.
HOLOGRAPHY MEANS WHOLE MESSAGE. 3D WITH LASERS. MAYBE SOMEDAY I'LL BE A HO-LOGRAPHER. (OK)
A CHORUS LINE WAS TERRIFIC. (KK)
NEW YORK IS AMAZING. I WISH IT WERE CLOSER TO WISCONSIN. (FL)

DAY 5

Radio City Music Hall. The Rockettes. A movie. Rockefeller Center.
THIS PLACE IS DEFINITELY NOT LIKE CINEMA 3 AT OUR MALL. (FL)
WHAT'S A MALL? JUST KIDDING. WE GO TO THEM SOMETIMES IN NEW JERSEY. I THOUGHT THAT WATCHING THE ROCKETTES WAS A REAL KICK. (KK)
I LIKED THE POPCORN. (OK)

DAY 6

Metropolitan Museum of Art.
THIS PLACE IS SO TERRIFIC. (KK)

INCREDIBLE. (FL)
I AGREE. (OK)

DAY 7

The Ks go with us. Statue of Liberty. American Museum of Immigration (located at base of statue), Ellis Island. Dinner: pasta at Bazzini's Restaurant.
A GREAT DAY. THE FERRY BOAT RIDE WAS FUN. WE LEARNED A LOT BUT IT WAS FUN ANYWAY. (KK)
I AGREE. (FL)
I WONDER IF THE STATUE OF LIBERTY USES UNDERARM DEODORANT. (OK)

Frank walks into the kitchen.

Looking up, I smile and say, "Hi."

What I really want to say is: So what's in the letter? Who wrote it to you? Does she really wear that perfume or does she use it as bathroom freshener? Is she pretty? Do you like her better than you like me?

I say none of those things, however.

Frank nods hello, walks to the refrigerator, opens it up, and looks for something, which he doesn't seem able to find.

He starts to walk around the room, looking in cabinets.

My mother told him to feel at home in the kitchen. Obviously he does.

"Are you looking for something special? Maybe I know where it is," I offer.

He shakes his head. "I don't think that what I'm looking for is going to be that easily found."

I figure out that he's not really looking for anything, that he's just doing something to be doing something— anything. When I get upset I act like that, but I didn't think anyone else did.

As he paces around the room, I realize that this is the first time that we've been alone. For seven days, the three of us have been Serendipities together.

When I don't know what to say, sometimes I chatter. This is one of those times. "So the summer's going to be fun, huh? We'll even get to go to the TV studio to watch *All My Children* being taped. It's really lucky that Dee, who lives in this building, is a lighting director on the show and that she's so nice and is getting us passes and giving us the tour. And then we can walk over to Lincoln Center, which is just around the corner from the studio, and then maybe we'll get the dreaded sushi meal over with. So what do you think?"

"Kendra," Frank says. "Have you ever been in love —really in love?"

I guess that when you ask Frank what he thinks, you've got to be prepared to hear what he's really thinking.

I want to seem sophisticated, really sure of myself, a woman of the world. Because sometimes I feel like such a kid around Frank.

"Yes," I say, and think of Jeremy. "Actually, no. I've been in strong like, but not in real love."

He starts to say something and we hear the door open.

It's too noisy to be parents.

O.K. and Ralph come in and head immediately for the refrigerator.

Our refrigerator is a giant magnet that draws people to it.

Bad timing for the kids to show up right now.

Actually, O.K. is known for his bad timing. He should have been born in the next century so that I wouldn't have to deal with him.

"Let's go for a walk." I look at Frank.

O.K. turns around. "Sure."

"No," I say firmly. "Just Frank and me."

O.K. falls to the ground. "Life is unfair. Alas. Alack. Woe is us."

Frank steps over his body. "Let's go."

We leave the apartment and go down in the elevator.

I'm dying to find out what Frank was going to say, but the elevator man starts talking. "So what do you think of those Mets? Aren't they the greatest? Have you had a chance to get over to Shea Stadium yet and see them play?"

"Joe." I sigh. "Frank just got here a little while ago, and anyway—not everyone is interested in a silly baseball game."

"Silly," Joe says. "Kendra. How can you say that?"

"I like baseball," Frank says. "You know, there were no sports things on the Scavenger list."

As we leave the building, I say, "That's because my family's idea of physical exercise is turning the pages of a book. My mother is also in the Worry Olympics. That burns a lot of calories."

Walking down the street, silently, I want Frank to start talking personally, but I'm not sure how to get him started again.

We pass a bag lady who has all of her belongings in a grocery cart. Talking to herself, she's searching through a garbage can.

"It's really sad. People like that," Frank says.

I nod.

In New York City, there are a lot of homeless people. It gets so that I don't even notice them, which is so awful to say. Now that Frank's here, I see them differently, through his eyes, and then through my own eyes and my own heart.

It is so sad.

My family always contributes to charity to help the homeless.

Lately I've been thinking about doing something on my own to help people out in the City. When school starts again, I'll be a volunteer tutor in one of the special programs in my neighborhood—as long as I don't have to help with math.

I'm beginning to realize how much I get from the City and now I want to give something back.

As we cross the street to go to Central Park, Frank points at a stretch limo. "That's the longest, biggest car I've ever seen."

I glance at it. Limos are another thing I hardly ever notice in New York City.

It's a strange city, with so much richness and so much poverty.

Frank says, "You know, back home I never saw a

limo. There are some big expensive cars, yes—but not something like that with a chauffeur. But then, back home I see a lot of tractors, and I haven't seen one here."

"I've never ever seen a tractor—not in person," I say.

We walk into the park.

Frank says, "Sometimes I feel like I've been dropped onto another planet. You'd feel that way too if you came to visit our farm. It's so different."

He gets quiet again.

"Let's go over there." I point to an empty space under a tree.

He nods and we sit down.

There's quiet again.

There used to be a lot of quiet times with Jeremy. However, I never had the feeling that much was going on in his brain when he was silent. With Frank, I get the feeling there are layers and levels.

I pick a blade of grass.

Finally Frank speaks. "Look, I don't know where to begin or what I want to say. This really isn't easy for me. Back home I don't have the kind of friends that I tell personal things to, so I guess I just have to start. So here goes." He takes a deep breath. "A lot has happened this year. Actually, some of it's been going on for a long time. For years my parents didn't get along. I knew they were heading for a divorce. In some ways, I hated it. Other times, I hoped for it. They'd fight over keeping the farm. Dad really loves it, but Mom wants to live in a big city. And even though they've both inherited a lot of money, the farm is becoming a drain."

Frank seems far away for a minute, and then he goes on. "Believe it or not, it gets worse. About a year ago, the doctors told my father that he had cancer. So for the past year he's been fighting that—going to hospitals, getting chemotherapy. My mother really helped him, stayed with him at the hospital. Now they think that maybe he has it licked and my parents want to get away and relax. Mom said that they want to rekindle the romance in their marriage." He makes a face. "Sometimes I think that's going to take an arsonist."

He smiles, and then gets serious again. "During that whole time, I was left alone a lot. They took all those trips to the hospital. There was this guy who was sort of a house sitter, but he really took care of the farm and mostly left me alone. It was good, because I got involved with someone and liked not being checked up on. Mary Alice is her name."

The one who writes S.W.A.K. all over her envelopes and pours tacky cheap perfume on them, I think, tearing a blade of grass into tiny strips.

Continuing, he says, "Mary Alice is three years older. She just graduated from high school and we got really close last year. I didn't feel so alone after we started going out. She's someone you can talk to and she listens—like you do, Kendra. And she's very mature."

While he goes on about how nice and pretty and wonderful she is, I try to sort out what I'm feeling. Jealous, maybe. Curious, yes. What did they do together? Hearing about Frank's "older woman" makes me feel like a kid.

Frank says, "Anyway, when the doctors told my father that he was all right, my parents came back and saw how serious it was between Mary Alice and me. They wanted it to end. They said that she was too old, too experienced, and that I was just a kid. They weren't around much for a year, and then they thought they could come back and run my life. There was a lot of fighting all the time. Finally, my mother took me aside and said that the fighting was upsetting my father too much and she was afraid it would make him sick again."

And I thought my mother gave guilt trips.

He looks very sad. "They said I should go to Europe with them—that they wouldn't leave me behind and that they wouldn't go if I stayed there. They said that they really needed the vacation. I didn't know what to do, you know. I'm only fifteen and that's not old enough to quit school and get a job. And I know that would be dumb to do. Running away wouldn't help, either. Mary Alice thought I could come live at her house, but her parents didn't like that idea."

I think about how much Frank's been through, what a survivor he is and also about how sad he is, and wonder what I can do to help him.

"So," he says, "we decided that I would stay in New York while they're in Europe and then, when we go back, we'll see what happens. They think the problem is going to vanish, but I still love Mary Alice, so the problem's not going to vanish."

He looks sad and angry. "I had to give in on this. What if my father dies? They're not sure that this isn't just remission, a break, and I wanted him and Mom to have a chance to try to be happy. I thought that if I'm reasonable, then when they come back, maybe they'll be reasonable too."

Frank just sits quietly, looking down at the ground.

Who would have thought that someone so cute, with so much going for him, would have so many problems.

I really do have to remember not to judge people so much on surface stuff. My parents are always telling me that.

I also think that I have to give up any thoughts that maybe Frank and I will be boyfriend and girlfriend.

Something tells me that this is the time to be his friend.

I think he really needs one.

"Now I know what the sportscasters mean when they talk about the agony of the feet. I don't ever remember walking around New York so much," O.K. says, taking a spoonful of Cheerios.

"That's the agony of de*feat.*" Frank laughs. "And we're definitely not defeated yet. In fifteen days, we've been to more museums than I've seen in fifteen years. And to lots of statues, monuments, restaurants—and let's not forget the ballet." Frank pretends to do a pirouette. He looks like Daffy Duck in toe shoes.

"I don't understand why you wouldn't let me eat popcorn during the performance," O.K. says, pouting.

"You are so uncultured," I moan.

"There's a kernel of truth in that, although O.K. may just be trying to be part of pop culture," Frank says.

O.K. continues, "Sometimes I think that Frank's favorite part of the museums are the shops where he buys postcards for Mary Alice."

Frank's face turns red as he tries to change the subject. "St. John the Divine. Riverside Church. They were so beautiful, so majestic."

"Yeah, and you sent Mary Alice cards from those places saying, 'I pray that we will soon be together.' " O.K. teases.

Frank blushes even more.

It's interesting to see a boy get so embarrassed.

"That's not true. I haven't even been writing every day." Frank sputters. "At least not lately."

O.K. and Frank start talking about the Museum of Broadcasting and all the great old shows we saw.

I tune out and think about the great show we're going to see today, my favorite, *All My Children.*

When I found out that Dee worked there, I almost died. Once she even let me hold one of her two Emmys for lighting the show, and I gave a make-believe speech for winning "Best Actress in a Daytime Series."

My fixation with the show started in the fourth grade when I got the chicken pox. I got hooked on it, and even now, when watching it means I use up all my TV time and can't see anything else, it's still my favorite. I tape them on the VCR and love finding out what's happening with the Martins, Tylers, Chandlers, Wallingfords, and Courtlands. I know them better than I know some of my own relatives.

When I saw that my parents listed a TV show on the Scavenger list, I just knew that the time was right. Dee had invited me before, but I'd always been too shy to go on my own.

"Eat up, guys. We're supposed to be at the studio by

eleven." I finish my breakfast and put my plates in the dishwasher.

O.K. holds an unpeeled banana and pretends it's a microphone. "It's only ten o'clock and already Miz Kendra Kaye is nervous about getting to her stupid soap opera, where we will witness love, hate, birth, death, and kidnappings. An ordinary day in ordinary households."

Frank laughs.

That creep. I didn't hear him be so joyful when O.K. was picking on him.

"Come on, guys. Hurry up," I plead.

They take their time.

It's obvious that they don't care as much as I do.

In fact, that is an understatement. They really don't want to go at all.

"You two, hurry up, please." I stamp my foot.

O.K. keeps kissing his own hand, saying stuff like, "Let me take you away from all of this. So what if I'm on trial for murdering my long-lost half-sister-in-law and for pickling her in a giant vat. So what if you are thinking of running off with the ex-husband of one of your former best friends, who is now engaged to the mayor."

Frank laughs and joins in. "If you don't go I will be compelled to inform your boss that you have been embezzling from him—that you have taken a six-year supply of paper clips, two cartons of typewriter ribbons, and eight million dollars from the petty cash fund."

Some days I'd like to strangle them both. "Look,

I'm leaving here in fifteen minutes. You know the rules. Each for all. Teach for all. We *all* go together."

"Be there or be square." O.K. uses a silly high-pitched voice.

I stomp out and go into my bedroom.

Looking under a pile of clothes, I find my makeup kit and apply a little more than usual.

I put on my new black halter dress, a pair of silver sandals, pile my hair up on my head, and wear a pair of silver hoop earrings.

Rushing into the living room, I see that the boys are still wearing jeans and T-shirts.

I decide to say nothing about their attire. If they want to look like grubs, there's nothing I can do about it.

Frank looks up at me and stands up. "Wow!"

"Yeech," O.K. says. "You look like an almost grown-up."

"Thanks," I say, ignoring the fact that O.K. didn't mean it as a compliment and not sure of what Frank meant.

Frank says nothing for a few moments but looks at me in a way that he never has before, and then he starts to walk over to be closer.

It makes me feel a little uncomfortable, but I kind of like it.

He steps back and then he says, "Mary Alice has a dress sort of like that, but it has straps and it's red."

So much for thinking whatever thoughts I had about the way he was looking at me.

Sometimes I hate Mary Alice, and then I remember that Frank and I are just friends.

"Come on." I grab my purse. "We have to be there by eleven."

"Do we turn into pumpkins if we're not?" O.K. grins.

"You turn into *squash!*" I yell, rushing out the door. "Let's go. And you better not do anything to embarrass me."

Miracle of miracles, the boys actually follow me.

We leave the apartment building, but not before Frank checks to see if the mail has arrived.

It has, but there is no perfumed letter. In fact, no letter at all from you-know-who.

We stop at our car, which is parked in front of our building with my father sitting in it. He's marking students' papers, waiting for his parking spot to become legal at eleven.

Another thing that Frank finds so weird and I'm just used to is alternate-side-of-the-street parking. Monday, Wednesday, and Friday, from eight to eleven A.M. one side of the street is legal, and on Tuesday, Thursday, and Saturday, it's the other side. Sunday is the day of rest—car rest. Frank's glad that he didn't bring his tractor into the city.

Another thing that throws Frank over the edge is the number of cars with signs that say "No Radio." The first time he saw one, he said that the car should also have a sign that says "No Hub Caps."

"We're on our way to *All My Children*," I tell my father.

"A little dressed up, aren't you?" My father smiles.

"We're on our way to *All My Children,*" I repeat.

My father thinks I should be wearing Dr. Denton pajamas and diapers.

"Kendra wants to be discovered," O.K. pipes up.

"Shut up," I say sweetly.

"Make me." O.K. grins.

"Have a good time at the show." My father goes back to grading papers.

"Bus!" Frank yells.

We race to catch the bus, just making it, and then transfer at Columbus Avenue.

The second bus is very crowded, so we stand up, holding on to the straps.

The bus stops short.

Frank loses his balance and grabs on to me to keep from falling.

He moves back, but not before we both blush.

For the rest of the ride, we hang on to the straps saying nothing.

Finally, O.K. speaks. "Sixty-ninth Street. This is where we get off."

Pine Valley, here we come.

I'm so excited. I feel like my heart is in my throat, like there are butterflies in my stomach, and like I'm standing on pins and needles.

Our family doctor would say it's a case of nerves.

My English teacher would say it's a case of overdone metaphors—or are they similes?

After all the years of watching the show, I can't believe I'm actually going to be seeing it live.

As we pass the back of the building, O.K. points. "It looks like someone's moving."

There are sofas, chairs, trees, and a car on the sidewalk.

"Dee says that's where they bring in the props," I inform them. "She also said that lots of people walking by try to take the stuff."

"It's probably the first time a tree has ever been mugged." Frank laughs.

"The trees probably don't get stolen much," O.K. says. "They're probably watch trees and have good barks."

I try to ignore them as we arrive at the front entrance.

"Ten more minutes." O.K. looks at his Mickey Mouse watch, then points to a group of people who are standing around. "I wonder what's going on."

Twenty or thirty people are just standing around, carrying cameras, talking to each other.

I decide to be brave and find out.

I spot two girls about my own age who look friendly.

I walk up to them. "Excuse me. Would you please tell me what's going on here."

They look very excited, practically jumping up and down. "This is where *All My Children* is filmed. It's the best show. My mother, aunt, and my cousin flew in last night from Montana and we're waiting to get a look at the actors. We've been waiting here since eight this morning and have already seen five."

And I thought I liked the show! I would never have *thought* of doing that, let alone actually do it.

Cousin Number Two is very breathy. "Everyone at school is going to be so jealous. It's so wonderful. And we even got two autographs."

She shows me the paper.

"Want my autograph?" It's O.K.

Quickly, I say, "Ignore him. He's my pain-in-the-neck brother."

"Cute," Cousin Number One says, patting O.K.'s head.

O.K. slinks away, back to where Frank's standing.

She laughs. "I knew that would do it. I've got a younger brother at home too."

It's so nice to be with two people who are not going to make fun of my loving *All My Children.*

Frank comes over. "Kendra. It's almost eleven."

"All right." I smile at the girls. "It was nice meeting you."

Walking away, I hear the breathy cousin say, "Now *that* is cute."

It makes me feel good to be seen with Frank, sort of like we're boyfriend and girlfriend, instead of boy friend and girl friend.

As we go through the revolving door, someone yells out, "Are you someone?"

I sure hope so, I think, but according to that person I'm probably not.

The second we get inside the door, the security guard comes forward. "May I help you?"

Nervously I tell him, "Dee said she'd put our names on the visitors' list. Kaye and Lee."

Oh, please, I think, don't let her have forgotten to put us on the list.

The guard smiles. "Kendra Kaye. Oscar Kaye. Frank Lee."

"That's us." I'm so relieved.

"Here are your passes. We'll page Dee now."

The guard grins. "Frank Lee. What a name. It's just like in *Gone With the Wind,* where Rhett says, 'Frankly, my dear, I don't give a damn.'"

Frank looks down at the floor. "I hear that all the time."

I wonder how I missed figuring that out. Probably it's better that I didn't, because he doesn't seem too happy about the guard's joke. How could his parents do that to him? I bet that if they'd had a girl she'd have been named Merry, as in "Merrily we roll along."

O.K. is staring at the television in the waiting room. "Could we please change this stupid show?"

I step on his foot and whisper. "This is ABC. That's an ABC show."

"So?" he asks.

I step on the child prodigy's other foot. "Don't be an embarrassment."

He whispers back, "If you break my feet, we'll have to go to the hospital instead of the show."

I back off.

Dee arrives, looking like she could be in front of the cameras instead of working behind the scenes.

As soon as we step through the door, I feel like it's the Fourth of July, Christmas, Chanukah, and my birthday all in one.

Even though no visitors are allowed on the set while they're taping, Dee says we'll still see a lot.

I'm already seeing a lot, because standing by the water fountain, like a regular mortal human being, is one of my favorite actors.

Be still, my heart.

Dee introduces us.

He smiles and says hello to all of us.

Then he looks directly at me and says, "Are you an actress or do you model?"

O.K., the creep, laughs and says, "She isn't even a waitress."

He thinks he's so cute saying that because in New

York City a lot of people who are trying to make it in show business have to wait on tables while they are taking lessons and going to auditions.

"She's only fourteen years old." Frank comes up behind me and puts his hands on my shoulders.

"Almost fifteen," I lie.

"Is this your boyfriend?" the actor asks.

"Just my friend," I tell him.

"A very good friend," Frank adds.

Dee and the actor smile at each other and then he says, "It was nice meeting all of you. Now I've got to go upstairs and go over my lines."

I say, "Nice meeting you, too."

As he leaves, I want to shout out, I wouldn't mind helping you study your lines!

Actually I wouldn't mind studying his lines.

As we walk down the hall, Frank whispers, "He's too old for you."

"Frank," I whisper back, "he was just being nice to me. What's your problem?"

"No problem," he says. "I just think, as your friend, I should watch out for you."

On the one hand, I feel good that Frank wants to look out for me. On the other hand, I think he should mind his own business. After all, he's still sending postcards to Mary Alice and pledging his undying love to her. On the other hand, I'm not sure, but I have a feeling that, strange as it seems, good old friend Frank is acting a little jealous. On still another hand, I realize that I should be an octopus if I have all these hands.

I wonder how old the actor is. He's too old for me

and probably involved with some other star, but it's nice to dream sometimes.

Dee's voice pulls me back into reality. "On the right is the wardrobe room."

I wonder who has worn what clothes and how the fur coat would look on me.

There's not much chance of my finding out, though, since there is a guard on duty.

"The makeup room."

Inside, one of the young actors says, "You've got to cover this zit, please."

"The hairdressing room." Dee points.

"I thought I'd get to see a hair getting dressed," O.K. says, and then points to the wallpaper. "Look at that."

I LOVE MY HAIRDRESSER is printed a zillion times on it.

"To the left are dressing rooms and the control rooms." Dee leads us forward.

"The control rooms are the ones in which to learn control. We should leave O.K. there." I giggle.

Dee smiles. "Some days we call them the out-of-control rooms. Actually, they're for everyone who puts the show together."

She leads us into a control room.

Frank whistles. "Talk about state-of-the-art equipment. We've dropped in on high-tech heaven."

"There must be twenty-five televisions in here." O.K. claps. "The major stations on all at once."

"No sound for any show but ours," Dee explains.

"Drats."

Dee ignores O.K.'s comment and introduces us to the other two people in the room. "This is Eric, my assistant."

He shakes our hands.

Eric is medium height, medium build, and seems very cheerful—a happy medium.

"This is Bonnie, who is the production assistant. She takes care of timing the show as well as the director's notes."

Bonnie smiles, waves, and goes back to her telephone call.

"Eric's going to give you a little tour while I continue to work. So have fun. Be careful to stay out of the way."

Eric leads us out.

As we exit, single file, I hear O.K. humming, "I Love a Parade."

"Shhh," I hear Frank say.

We pass behind some huge boards, which turn out to be the backs of sets.

Finally, we're in front of the sets. Pine Valley.

It's really so incredible. Some of it looks familiar. Some of it looks different. On TV, it seems like part of a set. There's even a staircase that goes nowhere.

There are people all over the place.

"This is a crowd scene," I say softly.

Eric nods. "There are five camera people and each has a cable kicker-puller."

"Ten." I start to add them up.

Eric continues. "Three boom guys. Each has a

pusher. Ten electricians—they're the ones with poles. Six prop guys."

"Thirty-two."

"Four carpenters, who move scenery and who raise and lower pipes. A couple of guys from the shop, who are repairing the scenery." Eric stops to take a breath.

I give up counting.

Eric still has more people to add to the list. "The scenic designer, two scenic artists, the wardrobe, hair, and makeup people, two to four people upstairs who run the lighting board, and later there'll be a nurse here because today there's going to be a baby shot."

"You shoot a baby?" O.K. gasps.

Eric laughs. "Of course not. That's what we call it when a child or baby is going to be in a scene. Look over here."

He points to a corner of the room where two of the actors are drop-kicking this really ugly doll.

"Children can only work a limited amount of time. So until the baby and nurse arrive, we use the doll."

Now one guy is throwing a wadded-up piece of paper and the other guy is using the doll as a bat.

Eric looks amused. "That's not a scene from the script. The guys are just letting off some steam. It can get a little crazy around here sometimes. Maybe they're practicing for the weekend baseball league. We have a team and play teams from other TV and Broadway shows. You should come watch sometime. It's in Central Park."

"I'll be there," I say.

"We have to continue doing the Scavenger Hunt." Frank looks at me.

I choose to ignore his comment and not to remind him how much he usually enjoys sports.

"There's the director." Eric points. The man yells, "Kill the coatrack!"

I've always known that soap operas have strange plots, but I've never heard of furnituricide.

"I can't kill the coatrack!" yells the prop man, or a person who must belong to SPCO, the Society for the Prevention of Cruelty to Objects.

I look at Eric, who says, "Lighting term."

"Cheat Langley," the director calls out.

Again I look at Eric.

"Langley has to be moved to a better position," Eric explains, as his walkie-talkie signals.

It's Dee. "Eric. Check the shot on Camera Five. It has no light."

"Looks like we missed that one." Eric turns to us. "I've got to go check on this. When you're ready, head back to the control room."

He leaves and the three of us keep out of everyone's way.

Frank moves behind me and puts his hands on my shoulders.

It's actually a very comfortable feeling. I could get used to it if I let myself.

A couple of the actors walk by, so close it's unbelievable.

We keep moving to make sure that we're out of everyone's way.

Each time Frank stays behind me with his hands on my shoulders.

My whole body feels different.

I'm not sure if that's because he's touching me or if it's because there is a love scene being rehearsed on the set.

I wonder what it would be like to kiss Frank.

I wonder whether he ever wonders what it would be like to kiss me.

I find myself wondering about a lot of what-it-would-be-likes.

O.K. finally says, "Enough of this mush. Let's go back to the control room."

I think, Just wait till you get a little older, O.K., kid. Then you won't think all of this is just mush.

Then I try to imagine O.K. making out with someone.

I don't know whether to laugh, cry, or throw up.

The thought does make me ready to return to the control room, even though I don't ever want to leave.

I don't want to overstay our welcome, either.

We go back to the control room.

"Good timing," Dee says. "I have a few extra minutes to talk. Did you have fun?"

"I loved it," I say.

"It's terrific." Frank smiles. "Once I worked backstage on a school play, but it was nothing like this."

"It was great." O.K. keeps looking at the twenty-five TV screens.

"Any questions?" Dee looks at us.

"What happens later?"

"After lunch break, there's a run-through. Everyone's here. The actors are ready in full costume. Then there's red chairs. That's what we call the notes. We used to sit in red chairs and discuss everything. We changed chairs, but the name stuck. Then we tape."

"How long does that take?" I want to imagine everything.

Dee laughs. "However long it takes to get the show in the can. The schedule says from four to seven P.M. but we run over a lot. Once we went to two A.M."

"But you've said that you have to be at work at three A.M.!" I gasp.

Dee nods. "It's not always as glamorous as some people think. I love my job and I make a lot more than I used to make when I was younger, but I do miss summer vacations. And it would be nice to live on a more normal schedule."

"It's hard work," Frank says, looking over at all the equipment.

Dee says, "It takes seventeen hours of work to get one hour of tape for one show and there are five a week on daytime television. For one hour of night, prime time, it takes seven days."

O.K. says, "I never knew it took so many people to put a show together. From now on, whenever I watch TV, I'm going to remember all of the people behind the scenes."

I sigh. "I'm going to remember every moment of this for the rest of my life."

"Terrific," Dee says, handing me a script. "This is

from today's show. It will help you to remember it even more."

I wonder if anyone has ever died from happiness.

"And here's something for each of you." Dee hands each of us a button that says ALL MY CHILDREN.

"Thanks." We all say it at once.

I look at her and bite my lip. "Dee, I know that this is really tacky after all you've already done, but do you think I could have two more buttons?"

"Sure. No problem." She hands them to me. "Look, kids, I have to tie up some loose ends here, so I'll meet you at the sushi restaurant in ten minutes."

"Do we have to go? Please don't make us. It's like eating straight out of an aquarium. Raw fish. We'll die," O.K. whines.

"We're going to get mercury poisoning and turn into thermometers." Frank clutches his throat. "I'm going to have to name my lunch Flipper."

Dee and I look at each other and laugh.

"Sushi," Dee says.

"Let's go and let Dee finish up." I grab the boys by the hands and then feel a little uncomfortable when I realize how holding Frank's hand is nothing like holding O.K.'s hand.

I stop holding hands.

"Let's make like a tree and leave," O.K. says.

We walk out of the control room, through the hall, and leave the waiting room through the revolving doors.

The crowd has gotten much larger.

The two cousins are still waiting.

I walk up and hand each of them an *All My Children* button. "Here. Have a great time in New York City."

"How did day seventeen of the Scavenger Hunt go?"
My mother comes into the living room, holding up
several pieces of mail. "How come you kids didn't
check the mail today? Here are a couple for you, Kendra."

We just sit on the sofa.

She puts the letters on the table and says, "Where's
O.K.? Is something wrong?"

"O.K.'s upstairs, visiting what's-his-face," I inform
her. "He's fine."

My mother looks at the letters, which I'm not picking up, and then she looks at us.

Sitting down on the chair, she says, "Want to talk
about it?"

I nod.

So does Frank.

However, neither of us begins talking.

I look at Frank.

He looks at me and then we both look straight ahead.

Finally, I speak. "We saw something today that was so awful and so depressing."

"So awful and so depressing," Frank echoes.

I continue. "Today, we went to Museum Mile. One of our stops, the last one, was the Jewish Museum."

My mother says, "I've always meant to go there."

Frank speaks. "You really should. The first two floors were really interesting. Since I'm Protestant and there aren't a lot of Jewish people where I live—actually hardly any—I learned a lot from the exhibits."

"Me too," I say. Even though I am Jewish, our family doesn't really practice. When I was thirteen, there were lots of Bar and Bas Mitzvah ceremonies and parties, but that's about it.

Frank looks at my mother. "And then we got to the third floor and went to this room on the right."

Again there is silence as we both remember.

Finally I say, "Mommy, it was so sad."

I hardly ever call her Mommy anymore, but somehow this time I want to, and I also want her to make me feel all better.

"There was this sculpture by a guy named George Segal," Frank tells her. "There were these two wooden poles with barbed wire across it and there was this one man standing there, made out of plaster. He looked so real."

My mother nods. "That's because Segal is known for making plaster casts of real people."

I bite my fingernail. "Lying behind him on the ground were ten dead people, all looking like they'd starved and been tortured, like someone just threw them there."

My mother's face is very sad. "My parents lived through that."

Frank holds my hand—a real friendship kind of holding, for both of us.

"The exhibit is called 'The Holocaust,'" I tell her. "And the information on the wall says that the bodies are placed like the Star of David." I feel my eyes tear. "Mommy. It was so awful to think that over six million people died."

She nods.

"I read about it in school," Frank says. "But it didn't seem so real before."

My mother says, "It is real. It did happen to Jews and to many Christians too. When I was growing up, my parents refused to talk about it. They were very young when they were taken to the camps and they lost their parents. They were always so worried, so afraid that something bad would happen. I grew up trying to make everything good for them, trying to be perfect."

"I remember them." I think of my grandparents who died while I was in elementary school. "I remember wondering why they had numbers tattooed on their arms, when no one else I knew had them."

"Why did they?" Frank asks.

"Because that's what the Nazis did to identify them." My mother looks like she's close to tears too.

"Once I took a pen and wrote numbers on my arm so that I would be more like them," I say. "And Nanny cried and made me wash it off immediately." It makes me so sad to think about it. "She said she never wanted to see it happen again."

My mother sits down and puts her hand on top of ours.

We all sit quietly for a while.

Then my mother says, "Nothing must ever happen like that again. We must remember that as long as any people are oppressed, so are we all."

I think about all the stuff we've studied in current events and realize how many problems there still are in the world and how someday the kids of today are going to be responsible for trying to make things better, if we aren't killed by a nuclear bomb first.

It's devastating just thinking about it.

My mother gets up, but before she goes she gives me a hug and kiss and then does the same for Frank.

After she leaves, he says to me, "Your mom is pretty terrific. I wish mine were more like her."

"I really do love her, but sometimes she can be such a nag."

"At least she pays attention to you all the time,"

Frank says, "not just when she thinks you are doing something wrong."

"She never lets up about my room." I make a face.

"Come on, Kendra." He grins. "There are jungles out there that have cleaner floors than your room does."

I pick up a pillow, reach over, and hit him on the head with it.

He tries to grab it and we end up wrestling—kind of.

Just as we get so close that it's almost like we're kissing, Frank backs away. "I think I'd better go write a letter now."

He gets up, goes behind me, and bops me on the head with a sofa pillow.

As he leaves, I throw one at him, just missing his head.

Then I sit there and think about all of the stuff that's gone on today.

I wish the gang were here so that I could discuss what's going on with me and Frank.

Enough is enough. I pick up my letters and open them up.

Hey Kendra —
I got my hair cut
really short.
I have a part in the
play, Sunrise at
Camp O'Bello.
I'm having a truly
terrific time Love, Ama

Kendra, Hi
My team won the
Camp Olympics.
You can't believe
how long my hair
has grown this summer.
I don't ever want to
leave camp Love, Akosua

J'aime
♡
Paris!
Au revoir,
Teri

Kendra Kaye
1592 W. 86th St
Apt 10D
NY, NY
10024

Boring. Boring. Boring.
Boring. Boring. Boring.
B O R I N G
Boring. Boring. Boring.
     "   "   "
Boringly and bored yours
♡ Shannon

KENDRA,

I'M IN LOVE !!!!!!!!!!!!!

So what's so new about that, you ask, since I'm always falling in love ?!?!?!?!?!?

Everything is new ——

Colin is so wonderful. He writes poetry. He's sensitive, smart and what's more — He has his driver's license ......and I'm not talking about a learner's permit ....
This boy doesn't need a learner's permit, not for anything.

I have so much to tell you — but not on the phone and certainly not on paper.

I can't wait to see you.

Love, Bethany

I'm not quite sure what Bethany's letter means. With Bethany it's hard to tell. She has what my Aunt Judy calls "a flair for the dramatic."

Life is certainly getting very involved. I wonder

whether, when caterpillars leave the cocoon and become beautiful butterflies, they have to deal with a lot of changing feelings and happenings. I think that butterflies have a much shorter life span than humans, although of course they do have a much longer wingspan.

"We're going to die," I say calmly, as we stand at the bottom of the steps that lead to the Roosevelt Island Tramway.

"You're such a wimpette." O.K. tries to push me forward. "Kendra, a tram is a simple mechanical conveyance designed to take people from one place to another—in this case from Manhattan to Roosevelt Island."

"The tram is a large box, held up by wires, going over the East River—a large body of water that we can fall into." I can feel myself getting a little hysterical.

Frank grabs me by my shoulders. "Kendra, you're usually so brave about things, willing to try anything."

"There are three things that I'm absolutely afraid of," I say. "Subways, the tram, and . . ."

"And?" O.K. looks at me. "Fill in the blank."

Blushing, I refuse to answer and go back to the original subject. "What if we're riding on the tram and there's a power failure and we get caught up in the air, hanging over the water without a net? What if the cables snap? What if a bolt of lightning hits us and the car melts down and we become encased in steel? What if . . ."

"I'm so glad you've inherited Mom's worry genes," O.K. says, interrupting me.

How dare he say that I've got my least favorite thing about my mother.

He continues talking. "What if Godzilla shoots up out of the water and gobbles up the car with us in it? That would really be an example of takeout food."

"People sushi!" Frank yells.

"There's a bridge from Queens where we can catch a minibus to take us to Roosevelt Island," I explain.

"The list says Tramway, not minibus." O.K. sounds exasperated. "Kendra, let's just get it over with. We'll get out there, come right back, and go to the United Nations."

I look at Frank. "I'll be your best friend if we don't do this."

"Yesterday you said you'd be my best friend if I sang 'Give My Regards to Broadway' while we were standing by Macy's department store at Herald Square. I did. So we're already best friends."

"We can be *best* best friends." I have no shame when it comes to trying to get out of some things.

Frank grabs my hand. "Let's go."

We climb up the stairs—thirty-four, to be exact— and get to the turnstiles, where we put in a token, the same kind used for subways and buses.

The three rolls of tokens that our parents gave us are almost gone.

We step into the tram.

It's so much cleaner than the subways.

Hanging from the ceilings are straps to hold on to. They look like stirrups, probably for King Kong's use when he captures this tram and sits on top of it.

There are a few places to sit, but they are all taken.

I look up at the ceiling again and see bars to hold on to. There's also a ladder. I don't want to think of what we might need a ladder for.

The doors slide shut.

No escape.

The driver says, "While standing, please hold on."

I put my arms around Frank's waist.

The tram starts.

Positively no escape.

"Look." Frank turns so that I can look out the window.

There are so many cars, trucks, buses, and people on the street. There are probably more people in ten blocks in NYC than there are in some towns.

Now we are above rooftops. Actually, it's pretty interesting, as long as I'm holding on to Frank.

We can look into some of the apartments as we pass by. On some of the rooftops there are parked cars. On others there are gardens. On still others there is garbage.

On one rooftop, there's a nude sunbather getting a very complete tan.

Frank covers my eyes.

In a minute, he uncovers them.

I look down.

The sunbather is no longer to be seen.

The East River is below us.

My heart is in my toes.

O.K. is getting facts from the driver.

"Roosevelt Island is three hundred yards off Manhattan's shore. It's two and a half miles long, eight hundred feet wide at its broadest point, and one hundred forty-seven acres."

I ask the important question. "How long does the ride take?"

"Five minutes. We're almost there," the driver says.

"How long before the tram makes the return trip?"

"It leaves every fifteen minutes. You have to get out and pay to reenter," he informs us.

We arrive.

I unlock my arms from around Frank's waist and we get out, pay again, and get back on again.

The tram is much more crowded for the return trip.

Some people are dressed very casually. Some look like they're going to work. Two people have brought on bicycles. Two women have carriages with babies in them.

I ask about the tram capacity and find out that it holds 125 people and can carry 21,000 pounds.

O.K., at my request, figures out how many pounds each person can be if the tram's filled to capacity. "About 168 pounds each."

As the tram starts, I do what I sometimes do on elevators—count the number of people, figure out their approximate weights, and decide whether to worry about safety.

I also look around and try to figure out if these are

people I'd want to spend a lifetime knowing if we were trapped in here forever. That's something I also do in elevators and buses.

The minutes seem like hours and then the ride's over. It wasn't so bad—not as long as I was holding on to Frank.

I remember how I felt when my parents announced that Frank was going to be staying with us, how I wondered whether he was going to be cute or doofy. Now my feeling that way seems so dumb. I'm learning how much more there is to knowing a guy—friendship, caring, trying to understand, not having to be perfect with each other.

O.K. tugs at my arm. "Stop daydreaming. We have to get to the UN, to get twenty foreign signatures. We've got a bus to catch unless you want to walk. It's about half a mile."

Bus, walking, trams—sometimes I wish I were like Dorothy in *The Wizard of Oz*. Then I could click my heels together and be anywhere. For Dorothy, once she figured it out, there were no worries about mass transportation, no crowds, no gridlock, when cars aren't able to move.

Grabbing Frank and O.K.'s hands, I click my Reeboks together.

We're still standing in the same place.

Obviously, I'm going to have to rely on reality, not magic.

United Nations, we're on our way.

METAL DETECTORS
STRAIGHT AHEAD

"I have to check your bag," the UN security guard tells me as we start to go through the detector.

"It's such a mess," I say, putting my purse on the table.

He smiles. "Everyone always says that."

"You should see her room!" O.K. says.

Stepping on my dear little brother's big foot, I think about how the guard has to look through bags filled with used tissues in them.

Gross. But I guess nothing can get in the way of international security.

My bag passes inspection and so do we as we go through the detector. No guns, no mace, no bombs, no machine guns on us.

Rushing to the tour ticket booth, O.K. says, "Dibs on getting the signatures."

"Sure," I say, relieved that I'm not going to have to be in charge of approaching strangers. "Just make sure that Frank and I are with you."

We go into the waiting area until our tour guide arrives.

People are standing around waiting, which is obviously why it's called the waiting area.

From the conversations I can tell that we have, as they say in old cowboy movies, hit "pay dirt." There are people here from all over.

O.K. goes up to one group of people, explains why we need signatures, and gets them.

"Five down. Fifteen to go." O.K. grins. "We have two from Austria and three from Germany."

Our tour guide arrives and our number is called.

One of the kids in the group asks, "What kind of dress are you wearing?"

"This is a sari. One size fits all. It's one long piece of material wrapped around and around," she explains. "I'm from Sri Lanka."

O.K. raises his hand, explains about our scavenger hunt, and asks for signatures.

"While he is getting the signatures," says the guide, "why don't you all say where you are from."

"China."

"Germany."

"Austria."

"England."

I wonder if they know my Aunt Judy.

"Botswana."

"Canada."

"France."

"Australia."

"Brazil."

"Holland."

Frank says, "New York . . . I mean, Wisconsin."

Very interesting.

As I say, "America, New York City," I hear a woman say, "Those two are such a cute couple."

O.K. tells her, "Yeah, and I'm their kid, Harold Square."

How embarrassing. There are reasons why I don't always see the kid as a real human being. It's because sometimes he acts like a real turkey.

The guide explains how the UN is an international zone, not part of New York, and we go through an area that shows what has and has not been accomplished by the UN.

Next we come to an exhibit dealing with Hiroshima and Nagasaki. The United States dropped atomic bombs on these Japanese cities during World War II.

It's really very upsetting.

There's a clock in a display case that stopped at eight fifteen, the exact moment that the bomb hit Hiroshima.

There are melted things in the cases—coins, soda cans, and cups fused together.

The guide explains that it would take about three thousand degrees Fahrenheit to melt those cups.

There's a statue with radiation burns on the back. We also see some drawings done by survivors.

It's awful to think about what it must have been like when the bombs hit.

I remember how I felt after the Jewish Museum as the tour continues.

We go into the discussion rooms. There are earphones, kind of like a language Walkman, that people can use to listen to the discussion in either Chinese, Spanish, Russian, French, and English, or the original language being spoken.

In one of the rooms there is an unfinished ceiling to symbolize the unfinished work of the UN.

As we walk through the halls, our group is talking about New York City.

"It's so dirty. All that grime and graffiti."

"Graffiti is a work of art."

"I'm afraid of the crime."

"So am I, but you can't stop doing things. You just have to be careful."

"There's so much to see here."

"It's a little overwhelming."

"It's so expensive."

"The subway is nothing like the London tube."

"Nor the métro in Paris."

"This is the place to be. There's no place else like it in the world."

"It's a nice place to visit, but I wouldn't want to live here."

I think about it. They're talking about my home. I realize that there are problems, but I really do love it.

The guide takes us to a mosaic of a Norman Rockwell painting.

As we look at it on the wall, she points out that the painter has put himself in it three times, as a young person, a middle-aged man, and as an old rabbi.

O.K. comes up next to me.

"That must have been a hard puzzle to put together."

We giggle and remember when he was much younger and saw a mosaic at the Metropolitan Museum and said that. Now whenever we see an artwork made of tiles someone in our family repeats what he said. It's a family tradition.

We walk through a few more areas and then complete our tour.

The guide points out all of the stores, where we can get souvenirs and things from other countries.

Saying good-bye to the people on our tour, we leave to go shopping.

I get postcards to send to the gang, also UNICEF cards.

Frank buys a bracelet for Mary Alice.

She really is lucky.

I look at Frank and O.K.

I'm pretty lucky too.

Break time.

I'm reading a book.

O.K. is upstairs visiting his friend, What's-His-Face.

And Frank is in his bedroom, reading the latest letter from You Know Who.

It's been a while since he's heard from her.

I really love the book that I'm reading. I'm rereading *A Proud Taste for Scarlet and Miniver* for about the millionth time.

Frank walks into the living room.

I smile at him.

He looks very upset, holding up his letter.

"What is it?" I jump up. "What's wrong. Is it bad news?"

He takes a deep breath. "It's a letter from Mary Alice. It's all over. She's dumped me."

"Are you kidding?" I look at him. "Are you all right?"

"No." He makes a face and shakes his head. "No. I'm not all right."

I want to reach out and hug him, but I'm not sure I should.

He throws the letter on the couch, looking as if he's going to cry or scream or both. "Read it. I hate her. I hate my parents. This is what they wanted to happen."

As I pick up the letter, he storms out of the room, saying, "I just want to be left alone for a while."

I don't know what to do.

Sometimes when I say I want to be left alone, I really don't want to, but I think that Frank really doesn't want to be bothered.

For a few minutes, I just sit, trying to figure out what to do.

I decide to pick up the letter and read.

Dear Frank,
~~This is probably one of the hardest letters~~
~~I'm sorry~~
~~I don't know how to tell you this~~
~~Hi. How are you?~~

SORRY
O
SLOPPY

It's over.
I'm sorry.
I know that we promised to be true to each other forever but I can't be there for you the way I used to be.

I've realized that I just can't give you what you need.

Also, I've met someone else, closer to my age. You're really mature for your age, but I need someone older.

Well, actually I didn't just meet him. I've known him for years.

His name is Walt Carter and he's a college junior.

Frank, I really do care about you and hope that we can always stay friends. It would have been hard this year, with me in college and you in the tenth grade.

Anyway, in all of your letters, you talk about all of the places you've been going. It doesn't sound like you've been stuck sitting home all summer doing nothing, which is the way it was for me until Walt. And all your letters talk about "Kendra and I did this" or "Kendra is" and "Kendra says."

I've spent a lot of time feeling jealous of her.

Even if nothing's happening, I wouldn't be surprised if something did.

```
Well, Frank, gotta go.
Love,                  Sincerely yours,
   Your friend,
```

Mary Alice

```
Mary Alice
```

P.S. I'm sending this letter without retyping it because I've already rewritten it five times.

"Kendra, are you reading that letter again?" My mother shakes her head. "Put it away. In the last three days, you must have read it a million times."

I put the letter down. "Well, it's interesting."

"Interesting." She laughs. "Kendra. Mary Alice was looking for an excuse so that she wouldn't feel guilty about breaking up with Frank. You know that you are not the real reason that she broke off with Frank."

"It was her fault. Look at how upset Frank is. He hasn't come out of his room except for meals and then he won't talk to anyone except when he has to," I say. "And he won't do the Scavenger Hunt anymore and now we're not going to finish it and be able to go to England."

My mother says, "I love the way you see everything

from your own viewpoint. What about just thinking about how bad Frank feels instead of worrying about your own trip to England."

"That's not fair!" I howl. "Of course I care about his feelings. I just miss being with him and doing the Scavenger Hunt."

"Remember how bad you felt when you and Jeremy broke up?" she asks.

"That was different," I argue. "Even though we both knew it wasn't working, I felt sad."

"Sad." She looks at me. "Honey, you might not want to remember, but you cried for days."

"But I'm a girl," I say. "Boys don't care so much about things."

"Kendra! I'm amazed at you." She looks at me as if I've just arrived from another planet. "How can you say that? You've seen your brother upset."

"That doesn't count. He's a little kid," I inform her.

"And your father shows his feelings."

"Yeah, but he's not a boy my age."

"Sometimes I wonder about you, Kendra. You seem to care so much about other people, to have a real understanding, to have heart. Then you say something like 'Boys don't care.' "

I've never told her that I don't understand boys at all, but she should realize it without my having to send her a telegram.

"Look," I say, "I don't think Frank's in his room crying. He's just upset. So what are you getting so annoyed about?"

She sighs.

"Anyway, I do care, Mom. What are you getting angry at *me* for? This is all Mary Alice's fault."

My mother sits down. "Look. It was no one's fault, honey. People break up. Frank and Mary Alice were too young to be so serious. It's good that she met someone new."

I smile. "Yeah, it probably is good."

"Kendra," my mother continues, "their breakup is for the best. I just want you to be careful now to remain Frank's friend. Nothing more."

"Mom," I say.

"Don't 'Mom' me." She smiles, but I can tell that she's very serious. "You're my daughter and I worry about you. You're only fourteen. I don't want to see you growing up too quickly."

Growing up too quickly to my mother can be anything from wearing too much eyeliner to having sex.

"Mom," I say again. "Don't embarrass me. Anyway, Frank's lived here for almost a month and nothing has happened. Nothing."

I do think of how I felt at *All My Children* and how kind of turned on I was when Frank and I were sort of wrestling, but I don't mention that to her. I'm not sure of what all of that means anyway. For someone my age, I feel pretty confused. Sometimes I wish I were doing more, like other kids I know, and other times I wish I were a little kid who says stuff like "Are you kidding? That sounds gross!" and "Yeech."

My mother says, "Honey, you know I think that you and Frank are terrific kids. I just want you to have your childhoods for a while longer."

There are some days when my mother says things that I just have to disagree with, even when I have this little feeling that she might be right. I think it must be some part of the brain that gets activated when a person hits puberty.

I start, "Then how come you're always saying that I should be a grown-up about stuff like cleaning my room, doing homework, and generally being more responsible?"

She laughs. "Because I'm the parent—that's my job."

I say, "Well, I'm the kid. So I have to try out new stuff to learn from—that's my job."

She gets up, pulls me up, and hugs me.

We stand that way for a while.

"Kendra," she says, resting her chin on my head. "I felt the same way when I was a kid, but couldn't even talk to my parents about anything. Yes, you do have to try new things. Just be careful of what they are and that you are ready to handle them. Life is very different from when I was growing up."

My father walks in, holding up tickets. "Guess what I've got? Tickets to the Mets game for all of us. This will cheer Frank up, get him out of his room."

Tickets to the Mets. That's enough to get me into my room and refuse to leave.

Watching grown-up men hit a little ball with a stick of wood is one of the more boring things in the world.

The only thing that is possibly more boring is math homework followed by a slide presentation of dissected mouse pancreases.

My father heads for the boys' bedroom.

"Mom," I whisper. "Do we have to go?"

"I like baseball," she reminds me. "Yes. We have to go. Your father spent good money for those tickets."

Where would he get bad money for the tickets, I want to ask, but don't. There are a lot of things that I think but know I shouldn't say. I have what my Aunt Judy calls a "smart-aleck mind." She says I got it from her.

Maybe I'll get lucky and Frank will refuse to go.

My father comes back into the living room.

He's smiling.

That's not a good sign in this case.

Strike One.

O.K. follows.

He's smiling too.

Another not-good sign.

Strike Two.

Frank is not smiling, but he is out of the bedroom.

Three Strikes and I'm out.

Out of the house and on my way to a Mets game.

"What are all these people doing in the parking lot?" I look around.

"Parking." O.K. grins.

"Cute." I step on his foot.

My father explains. "People start arriving hours before the game. They bring dinner and have a tailgating party."

People are barbecuing, sharing and trading meals with each other, watching portable TVs, and just generally hanging out.

Back in Manhattan kids hang out and socialize in certain areas. Some are on the front steps of the Metropolitan Museum of Art. Some always meet in Rockefeller Center. In each area of the city, groups of kids have places to meet and greet each other.

In the borough of Queens, people obviously use Shea Stadium. The major difference is that there's a place to go—the game—after hanging out.

"I'm hungry," O.K. whines.

"You just ate," my mother says, holding on to his hand.

He tries to let go.

"Hold on, O.K. We're in a big crowd." She takes his hand.

"Mom, I'm not a baby anymore," he whines again.

"You'll always be a baby to her," I inform him. "Especially if you continue to sound like one."

"Don't start, you two." My father buys three pennants from one of the vendors standing by the gate. "Here. For each of you—a souvenir. Now if you get lost, here's where we meet. Right by the ticket sales area. Only don't get lost."

Ever since I can remember, whenever we go anywhere, my parents always specify a place to go if we get lost.

When O.K. and I were little, we used to have to wear a harnesslike thing so we wouldn't wander off on our own.

It's good that the things aren't manufactured in preteen and teen sizes or we'd probably still have to be wearing them. Sometimes, even now, it feels like I have an invisible one on my body.

My parents and O.K. lead the way. Frank and I are close behind. It really would be easy to get lost here.

As we walk up the ramps, with crowds of people all around us, I turn to Frank and say, "Are you going to be tall, dark, handsome, and silent for the rest of your life? Or are you just practicing to be a mime?"

He actually smiles. He doesn't say anything, but there is a smile.

"I've had it," I say. "Talk. Don't you want to let me know what's going on?"

He shrugs.

"You are not easy." I grab his arm. "I am not giving up on this. Look, we're friends. Friends help each other."

As we get closer to the stand, Frank points. "Look."

People are having their pictures taken with cardboard cutouts of some Mets players who are probably the most famous ones—but how should I know who they are?

"Do you want to do that?" I ask.

"No," he says. "I just thought it was interesting."

I grin. "He walks. He talks. Wind up the Frank doll and he actually acts like a real human being."

Frank puts his hand on my head, messes up my hair, and says, "We'll talk about the serious stuff later. Now I just want to relax, OK?"

"All right," I say, because with Frank I've learned that patience is important. He's kind of like my friend Shannon that way. Neither finds it easy to talk about what's bugging them.

We walk into the stands and some guy leads us to our seats.

This place is gigantic. Down behind the playing field is a huge screen that keeps showing information about the players and a whole lot of other stuff, including commercials. Commercials—how gross. Somehow it doesn't seem right to pay to go to a game and have to look at ads. Someone on the field sings the National Anthem and the game begins.

Actually, it's pretty interesting.

Not the game, but what goes on in the stands.

Some people are wandering around dressed in strange costumes. One guy has on a mask and an outfit with a cape. The insignia on his shirt says SUPERMET. A few have face makeup on, like clowns or something. They act sort of like cheerleaders. As they walk through the bleachers, I try to imagine what they do in the real world. I wonder if this is the one time in their lives that they feel like celebrities. I bet it would be interesting to interview them to find out the real story, but maybe not. This might be the most interesting thing that they do in their lives.

"Peanuts. Popcorn. Beer. Hot dogs. Sodas. Ice Cream. Buttons. Pennants. Programs," the vendors are all screaming out.

"I'm hungry," O.K. says.

When the hot dog guy comes by, Frank buys some for all of us. "A peace offering," he says. "Thanks for putting up with me."

"Is this Let-Me-Be-Frankfurter with You?" I ask.

He takes a dab of mustard and puts it on my nose.

My parents groan and blame each other for giving me the punning gene.

"Since Kendra makes the jokes up, I guess that means she has designer genes," O.K. says.

My parents groan again.

"Look." Frank points to the bleachers above us and to the left. Everyone in the entire section has stood up, waved their hands, made a weird noise, and sat down, and then the next section does the same.

"That's called The Wave," my father explains.

Some guy on the field hits a home run, someone wearing a blue and orange uniform.

With three men on and the homerun, it's four to nothing.

A giant apple comes up.

The large screen flashes fireworks.

It's actually pretty exciting.

I find myself standing up and screaming with everyone else.

We sit down and get Cokes.

A lot of the game seems to be spent cheering and eating.

Actually, there are worse ways to spend a day.

Then it gets boring.

There are lots of players striking out.

Boring. Truly boring.

I look around at the people in the stands. That's more fun.

Frank leans over and says, "Let's go for a walk. We can talk."

Patience pays off.

As we get up, I say, "We'll be back soon."

"I want to go, too." O.K. stands up.

"No," I say, Frank says, and so do the parents.

O.K. sits down again and pouts. "Why does everyone get to do stuff but me? How come Kendra and Frank can do what they want?"

That little creep. For the whole summer he's been included in almost everything.

As Frank and I start to leave the bleachers, my father buys the little nerdface an ice cream, which cheers him up.

My mother says, "Take the ticket stubs with you. Don't forget which entrance to take. Don't get lost."

Where does she think we are, in a revolving restaurant?

Frank and I go out and stand by a pole.

There seem to be millions of people out here buying food and souvenirs from the concession stands and going to the bathrooms.

There are long lines to the men's rooms. How strange. In most places, there are longer lines to the ladies' room. Must be all the beer.

I wait.

Finally, Frank speaks. "Kendra. I'm sorry I haven't talked to you for a while but I had a lot to think about, get straight in my head."

"You could have talked it out with me," I say. "Maybe I could have helped straighten it out."

He smiles. "I know you would have helped. It was good knowing that, but I needed to work it all out myself before I could talk about it. That's my style."

It's certainly not mine. The second anything goes wrong, I want to talk to someone and agonize about it. I guess my style is much more public than Frank's. My friends are a lot more like I am, except maybe Bonnie, who keeps more to herself.

"I guess you're pretty devastated by Mary Alice's letter."

He nods.

I wait for him to say something.

It takes a while and then he says, "I guess I really knew it couldn't work out. Mary Alice was the first girl I really cared about."

He pauses, thinking. "The summer between eighth grade and ninth, I changed. I got much taller and I worked hard on the farm. All of a sudden, there were muscles. My voice was different. I had to shave. Nothing was the same."

Another caterpillar, I think. I've never thought about boy caterpillars before.

He continues. "In the fall, school started and all of a sudden it was different. Inside, I was the same kid, but then this stuff started happening. My father's illness. High school. Being more popular. Girls."

I can understand that.

"And then I needed math tutoring. Mary Alice, who was in Future Teachers of America, was assigned to help me." He grins. "The rest, as they say, is history."

I can't help it. I feel jealous of Mary Alice.

He continues. "You know, it wasn't always easy. She had the driver's license. So did all of her friends. I didn't really fit in with them. I never had any of the same classes. Some were on the Varsity team. I was Junior Varsity. One of her friends had even baby-sat for me when we were younger. But Mary Alice and I had something special. After all the time being alone on the farm, I had someone to talk to, someone who cared about me, who I cared about."

He blushes. "There were other reasons that it was special too."

I'm not so sure I want to hear about those reasons.

Frank continues. "I don't want you to think it was perfect. Mary Alice wanted us to be together all the time, and sometimes I like to be alone. We didn't agree on everything, but she helped me feel good about a lot of stuff during a really rough time."

I begin to think of Mary Alice as a person, one who I might actually like.

Frank puts his hands on my shoulders. "Kendra. It's more than that. Being on the farm was lonely. I'm an only child. My parents don't always get along, and who knows what it's going to be like when I return. This summer has been great. I really feel close to you and your family. You're probably the best friend I've ever had. You have so much energy. You like to try new things and you're so much fun to be with. The summer is almost over and I'm going to have to go home. Knowing that Mary Alice was going to be there made it all easier."

"Maybe you can stay with us, go to school here," I say softly.

He shakes his head. "My parents would never allow that."

Somebody accidentally pushes me and I move closer to Frank.

He says, "I talk to you more than anyone else in the world. I'm really going to miss you."

"Me too." I realize how special he is to me.

I look up at him.

He leans down and kisses me very lightly on my lips.

I return the kiss.

We move closer and kiss again—not so lightly this time.

Our arms tighten around each other.

He's holding on to me as if he's never going to let go.

It's like we're the only two people in the entire stadium—like someone's hit another home run and there's a fireworks display.

He kisses me again and then we just stand there, holding on to each other.

Finally, Frank moves back and puts his hands on my shoulders.

"Keeping me at arm's length," I say.

He looks at me and nods. "I guess so. Wow, somehow I had a feeling it would be like that."

So he has thought about it, too.

Shaking his head, he says, "I have to tell you something."

Suddenly I get very nervous.

"My parents made me promise two things this summer," he says. "One. I wouldn't run away and return to Wisconsin. Two. I wouldn't get involved romantically with you over the summer."

"And you promised?"

He nods. "Who knew?"

I grin. "Do you always keep your promises?"

He pulls my hair away from my eyes. "In this case, yes. Kendra, every day of the summer we've gotten more involved, closer. In some ways getting to know you has been easier because we weren't boyfriend and girlfriend."

I nod. Even though Bethany's always been my best friend, Frank has become that too, but differently.

"This is very confusing," I say.

"For me too," he agrees.

"Look. I need to know something." I stare at him. "Is what's happening between us because you're on the rebound, ending with Mary Alice? Am I just someone to kiss?"

"No," he says impatiently, and then pauses. "I don't think so. That day at *All My Children* and lots of other times I've found myself thinking about wanting to be closer, wanting to touch you."

We're both silent for a minute.

"So what's next?" I think aloud.

He shakes his head and smiles. "Actually, I want to kiss you again."

"Me too." I grin, but take a step back.

"I'm never going to promise anything ever again," he says. "But you know something?"

"What?"

"Maybe this is best for now. I only promised for the summer."

"How many weeks to the fall?" I ask, grinning.

Frank says, "Kendra Kaye, you are my best friend. Friends are forever. People you date aren't always."

I think of Jeremy. Of Mary Alice.

"Look," I say. "Maybe we should just wait and see. Give everything a chance to work itself out."

He nods.

I'm not sure if I'm saying this because I totally believe it or if it's because I'm a little scared by how strong my feelings were when we kissed each other.

All I know is that I've learned that boys and girls can be friends, that we're not from different planets after all.

For now, maybe friendship with Frank is best. Someday it may change, but I don't want to take a chance on losing what we have.

Getting kissed like that sure was interesting, though.

It's probably not a good idea to ask Frank for tutoring to prepare me for tenth grade.

"We'd better head back in," Frank says. "Your mother will be sending out a search party soon."

I smile.

We walk back into the bleachers area.

He says, "Starting tomorrow, we better get back to the Scavenger Hunt and make up for lost time."

I think about it.

Even if we do lose, I've still won because I've learned so much.

However, I don't want to lose the trip.

I really want us to go to England.

Tomorrow we start making up for lost time.

"Stop splashing!" I want to strangle O.K.

"I'm not splashing. I'm flicking." O.K. puts his hand back into the fountain and flicks water at me.

I debate dunking the little creep in the fountain in the middle of Lincoln Center but decide against it. We want to have pictures of our last day of the Scavenger Hunt and it would look suspicious if O.K. looked like a drowned rat.

And there would be too many witnesses. People are going into Avery Fisher Hall to hear the Philharmonic Orchestra play. There are people going to see a play at the Vivian Beaumont Theater. Others are hanging out waiting to hear the concert we're going to. The Allegro Café and the concession stands are also crowded.

So I decide to let the little creep live. I've gotten kind of fond of him over the summer, even though I wish he didn't have to hang around Frank and me all the time.

Finally, I've figured it out. The Scavenger Hunt part "each for all," where we had to do everything together, was part of a parental plot to keep Frank and me from spending too much time alone.

Parents can be so sneaky sometimes.

"We've done everything on the Scavenger Hunt but the concert and we go to that in half an hour," Frank says, as we sit on the fountain ledge. "I can't believe that we actually did it. If only we could go back and see some of the things again."

I agree, remembering all of the fun we've had.

"How about the Planetarium?" O.K. giggles.

It's my turn to be a water flicker, getting him right in the face. "Never again will I take you there! How could you ask the guide what it means to moon."

O.K. grins. "How am I going to learn if I don't ask questions? And you and Frank really liked the planetarium. When the lights went out I saw you holding hands."

"Being there made me starry-eyed," I say.

"It was heavenly." Frank looks at me and smiles.

I can feel myself start to blush. Fortunately it doesn't show since I got sunburned.

There's so much to say to Frank and so little time.

Even if there were all the time in the world, I'm not sure that I could say what I really feel, because I'm not sure of what it is that I want to say or how to say it.

By the time I figure it all out, he'll be gone.

His parents will be returning from Europe tomorrow and then the next day they'll all be going home to Wisconsin.

My life will never be the same.

"O.K." I pinch him on the arm. "Why don't you go get yourself an ice cream?"

Looking at Frank and then at me, he bargains. "All

right. It's going to cost you, though. You have to pay for the ice cream."

Frank and I both hand him money at the same time.

"A profit. This will also pay for snacks for the concert." He rushes to the concession stand.

Frank moves closer.

He looks so cute.

"I don't want you to go," I say.

"I don't want to go." He holds my hand.

We sit silently for a few minutes and then I say, "It won't be forever. We'll all be going to England together."

He laughs. "All together! Your parents, my parents, O.K.—the whole group. I wouldn't be surprised if they tried to bring Rover, my cow, for me to take care of so that we'd never have a chance to be alone."

"Taking a cow to England is a lot of bull." I try not to get too serious and depressed.

"You can tell that you've never been on a farm." He takes my other hand.

"I could be your very own Fresh Air Fund kid," I offer.

"I'm really going to miss you." Frank looks sad.

I lean over and give him a kiss, which he returns.

We lean back and look at each other.

"I'll write to you every day," I let him know.

"Promise me." Frank holds my hands. "Don't fall in love with anyone else until I see you again."

I look into his eyes. "I promise. Now you promise too."

He does.

Just as we get ready to kiss again, O.K. returns, clutching a large ice cream cone. "I tried to stay away for a long time, but then it got boring being all by myself."

I look at him.

He's wearing the green foam rubber Statue of Liberty crown that we got this morning on our search for tacky souvenirs. And he's carrying the ice cream cone, which is dripping all over his hand.

Picking up my Polaroid camera, I take a picture.

"Let's get one of all of us together," Frank suggests.

O.K. runs up to this nice-looking older couple and asks them to help us.

They smile and agree, saying stuff like "Isn't he cute?"

O.K. stands on the fountain ledge wearing his crown and holding up the ice cream as if it's a torch.

Frank stands with his arm around my shoulder.

With my right hand, I hold up a replica of the Empire State Building, which doubles as a salt and pepper shaker. My left hand is around Frank's waist.

The couple snaps three pictures, one for each of us, and gives back the camera.

I know where my photograph will go—on my dresser mirror so that I'll see it every day. Maybe I'll call the picture of Frank and me and O.K. "Two Butterflies and a Preteen Caterpillar," or maybe on days when O.K. and I have a fight, "Two Butterflies and a Preteen Slug." Actually I'll always think of it as "The Serendipities." The definition of "being able to make fortunate discoveries accidentally" was right for us.

One of the things that I've learned is that I'm much better off being a person than a butterfly, although there are going to be times in my life when I may have to wing it.

"Kendra, it's time." Frank grabs my hand and pulls me away from my thoughts.

It's time—not to wing it, but to get to the concert.

As we rush to the bandshell, I think about how our Serendipity summer is almost over.

I hate to think about what it's going to be like when Frank leaves.

He's gone.

Life will never be the same.

I sit in the kitchen eating Aunt Judy's favorite breakfast, Diet Pepsi and M&M's plain. When she lived in New York City, I used to stay with her a lot and that's what we'd eat.

My mother disapproves.

However, *she* is still asleep.

So are my father and brother.

Somewhere out there Frank is awake—on the way to LaGuardia Airport with his parents.

Last night, after dinner at Tavern-on-the-Green, where it all began, we said good-bye, and then he and his parents went to the hotel.

I look out the window.

The sun has come up, just as if life has not changed.

Some of the bad news is that the Scavenger Hunt is over.

The good news is that my parents are going to get me student memberships to the museums that I love so that I can go whenever I want.

I realize, after all of the things we've done this summer, how much New York City means to me. I want to continue going to as much stuff as possible and eventually, when I grow up, I want to live and work here on my own.

More of the bad news is that Frank is gone and New York won't be the same without him.

I pour all of the M&M's out on the table, separate them into colors, and then make designs with them.

Every once in a while, I pop an M&M into my mouth and take a sip of soda.

Just as I'm finishing making an M&M garden scene, my mother comes into the kitchen.

She looks at the table and goes over to the stove to make a cup of coffee.

Without a word, she takes out a bowl and pours Cheerios and milk into it. Then she puts sliced bananas on top and places the bowl in front of me.

Still without talking, she sweeps the M&M's into a bowl, takes them away, removes the Pepsi, and gives me a glass of orange juice.

She finally speaks. "I miss Judy too."

I stare down at the bowl of Cheerios and remember how, when I was little, my mother used to string them into necklaces, which I then ate whenever I got hungry.

"You're up early," she says. "Are you all right?"

"Yup." I take a spoon and try to drown a piece of banana. "Nope."

She picks up a handful of M&M's and puts one on each of my banana slices.

Sometimes it's hard to predict what my mother is going to do.

"Want to talk about it?" She takes a sip of coffee.

"There's not much to say." I flip over a piece of banana and scream, "M and M overboard!"

My mother starts to laugh and tries not to spit the coffee out of her mouth.

She's almost successful.

As she wipes the coffee dribble off her chin, she says, "Kendra."

I shrug. "So I'm a little depressed."

"Having Frank here was nice." My mother adds milk to her coffee.

"I miss him," I say.

"Me too." She stirs the coffee and milk. "A lot of days he got up before you and O.K. did and came down here. We talked about things before I went to work."

"I didn't know that."

She takes another sip of coffee.

I debate trying to say something so funny that it makes the coffee come out of her nose but decide not to do it.

She continues. "We had some good talks. I tried to help him work out some of his problems. He even helped me to be more understanding about you."

"In what way?" I put down my spoon.

"To let go a little, to not be so nervous about everything. To give you a little space to grow up." She grins. "Haven't you noticed?"

"Yes," I say softly. "Thanks."

"I'm trying not to be as worried about you kids as my mother was about me and Judy, but I was brought up with a lot of fears and it's hard to get over them. It's funny. Judy and I are so different in some ways and so alike in others."

"Like me and O.K.," I tell her.

"Yes," she agrees. "Like you and O.K. You know, when you were a little baby I used to call Frank's mother a lot. She was older, her baby was a little older than you, and she gave me some good advice. Kendra, when you and Frank were babies, his mother and I would talk on the phone about how great it would be if you two got married someday, how we would be in-laws."

"Did you really? Maybe we should elope and make your dreams come true." I giggle.

"Make us in-laws and we'll make you outlaws." She shakes her finger at me. "You're far too young."

"Not too young forever," I remind her.

She's quiet for a few minutes and then she says, "You and Frank didn't get too serious about each other, did you?"

No miracle worry-free transitions for my mother.

I ease her fear. "No."

"I hope that you don't mind if I ask you another question." She looks at me. "You and Frank didn't promise to go steady, did you?"

She sounds like an old sixties movie, like *Gidget Goes to Hawaii,* only it's *Kendra Goes Steady.*

"No." I raise my hand as if to swear in court. "I promise we didn't."

"Good." She gives out with one of her sighs.

"In fact," I continue, "because of getting to know Frank, I understand boys better, and when I get back to school, I'm going to try to get to know some of the guys better as human beings."

"That's a good step." My mother smiles.

I debate asking her what the steps lead to but decide not to because she might freak.

O.K. runs in. "Good morning. My room's so empty without Frank and his stuff in it. Where is he? I want him to come back. How come there are M&M's floating on Kendra's bananas? How come she gets to eat that and I never do?"

The phone rings.

I race for it.

Even though it's very early in the morning and none of my friends call at this hour, I still run to the phone.

It's a reflex action. When a phone rings, I run for it.

Sometimes a pay phone on the street will ring and I'll answer it, hoping that it's for me.

"Hi," I say. "Who is this?"

"Frank Lee, my dear, I do give a damn." His familiar voice makes me so happy.

"Where are you?" I shriek.

"At the airport. We ran a little late. There was a lot of construction on the highway. There're only a few minutes before we board. I just have to tell you something."

"Yes." My voice is very breathy.

"Go to the linen closet. Look at the third shelf from

the bottom. Check underneath the Smurf sheets. There's a present for you there."

"For me?" I only wish I could hug him.

"For you," he says.

I can hear the voice in the background saying that it's the last call for boarding. I can also hear Mr. Lee's voice telling Frank to hurry up.

We say good-bye.

My family looks at me.

"Frank called to say good-bye," I inform them.

"And you didn't let me talk to him," O.K. whines.

"He had to get on the plane," I explain. "Look, I'll be back in a few minutes."

I leave the kitchen.

The gift is right where he said it would be.

I pull out a long jewelry box, tear off the wrapping paper and ribbon.

Opening it, I find a silver identification bracelet.

On one side, it says SERENDIPITY SUMMER.

I turn the bracelet over. Etched in tiny script writing, it says, "Remember Me to Harold Square."

I give the bracelet a little kiss and then put it on my wrist.

"Don't worry, Frank," I say softly. "Harold won't forget you and I won't forget you either."

I can't wait until we go to London and see Harold's English cousin, Trafalgar Square.

We will soon be there.

THE FACTS HUNT

1. **Q.** HOW MANY BLOCKS ARE THERE IN A MANHATTAN MILE, IF YOU ARE GOING UPTOWN OR DOWNTOWN (NORTH–SOUTH)?
   A. 20 BLOCKS TO A MILE
2. **Q.** WHY WAS "THE DAKOTA" APARTMENT BUILDING GIVEN ITS NAME? GIVE THREE FACTS ABOUT THE BUILDING.
   A. BUILT IN 1884 ON WEST 72nd ST., IT WAS ONE OF THE FIRST APARTMENT BUILDINGS IN THE CITY. LOCATED FAR FROM WHERE THE MAJORITY OF PEOPLE LIVED, IT WAS SAID THAT IT WAS LIKE GOING TO "THE DAKOTAS."
3. **Q.** WHAT IS NEW YORK CITY'S NICKNAME?
   A. THE BIG APPLE
4. **Q.** HOW LONG IS MANHATTAN?
   A. 13.4 MILES
5. **Q.** HOW WIDE IS MANHATTAN AT ITS WIDEST POINT?
   A. 2.3 MILES
6. **Q.** WHERE IS THE WIDEST PART OF MANHATTAN ISLAND?
   A. FROM RIVER TO RIVER AT ABOUT 87th ST.
7. **Q.** HOW MANY BOROUGHS ARE THERE IN NEW YORK CITY?
   A. FIVE: MANHATTAN. THE BRONX. BROOKLYN. QUEENS. STATEN ISLAND.
8. **Q.** WHICH OF THE FIVE BOROUGHS IS THE

ONLY ONE CONNECTED TO THE AMERI-
CAN MAINLAND?

A. THE BRONX

9. **Q.** WHAT ABOUT THE REST OF THE BOR-
OUGHS?

A. ALL OF THE OTHERS ARE ISLANDS OR
PART OF LONG ISLAND.

10. **Q.** IN WHICH DIRECTION DO AVENUES
RUN?

A. NORTH–SOUTH

11. **Q.** IN WHICH DIRECTION DO STREETS
RUN?

A. EAST–WEST

12. **Q.** WHEN WAS NEW YORK DISCOVERED?

A. IN 1524, GIOVANNI DA VERRAZANO, AN
ITALIAN SERVING FRENCH KING FRAN-
CIS I, DISCOVERED NEW YORK BAY.

13. **Q.** WHEN DISTANCES FROM NEW YORK
CITY ARE GIVEN, WHAT MANHATTAN LO-
CATION IS USED?

A. COLUMBUS CIRCLE

14. **Q.** ON WHAT STREET WILL YOU FIND THE
NARROWEST HOUSE? AFTER VISITING
IT, GIVE THREE FACTS ABOUT IT, IN-
CLUDING ITS WIDTH.

A. 75 1/2 BEDFORD ST. IT WAS BUILT IN
1873. IT IS ONLY 9 FT. 6 IN. ACROSS. THE
POET EDNA ST. VINCENT MILLAY LIVED
THERE IN 1923 AND 1924.

15. **Q.** WHAT IS THE NAME OF THE AWARD
GIVEN TO BROADWAY PLAYS AND HOW
DID IT GET THAT NAME?

A. THE TONY AWARDS, NAMED AFTER AC-TRESS/DIRECTOR ANTOINETTE PERRY.

16. **Q.** WHAT IS THE NAME OF THE AWARD GIVEN TO OFF-BROADWAY PLAYS AND HOW DID IT GET THAT NAME?

A. THE OBIE AWARDS, OB FOR OFF-BROAD-WAY

17. **Q.** WHAT ARE THE NAMES OF THE TWO LIONS IN FRONT OF THE MAIN BRANCH OF THE NEW YORK PUBLIC LIBRARY AND WHO GAVE THEM THESE NAMES?

A. PATIENCE AND FORTITUDE WERE NAMED BY FIORELLO LaGUARDIA, WHO WAS ONCE THE MAYOR OF NEW YORK.

18. **Q.** WHAT DOES SoHo MEAN? AND NoHo?

A. SoHo MEANS SOUTH OF HOUSTON. NoHo MEANS NORTH OF HOUSTON. HOUSTON IS A STREET THAT RUNS EAST–WEST ACROSS LOWER MANHAT-TAN. IT'S PRONOUNCED "HOWSTON."

19. **Q.** WHAT DOES TRIBECA MEAN?

A. TRIBECA MEANS TRIangle BElow CAnal. CANAL STREET ALSO RUNS EAST–WEST ACROSS LOWER MANHATTAN, BELOW HOUSTON STREET.

20. **Q.** HOW MANY ACRES IS CENTRAL PARK AND WHAT ARE ITS BOUNDARIES?

A. 840 ACRES. THE BOUNDARIES ARE BE-TWEEN 59th STREET AND 110th STREET AND BETWEEN FIFTH AVENUE AND CEN-TRAL PARK WEST.

21. **Q.** NAME FIFTEEN IMPORTANT FACTS THAT YOU LEARN WHEN VISITING THE PARK.

A. (1.) IT'S 2½ MILES LONG.

(2.) IT'S ½-MILE WIDE.

(3.) IT WAS DESIGNED BY FREDERICK LAW OLMSTED AND CALVERT VAUX.

(4.) FROM MAY TO SEPTEMBER, THERE IS STORYTELLING AT THE HANS CHRISTIAN ANDERSEN STATUE.

(5.) THE SHAKESPEARE GARDEN IS AT THE W. 81st ST. ENTRANCE. THERE ARE PLANTS, FLOWERS, HERBS, AND SHRUBS THAT ARE MENTIONED IN SHAKESPEARE'S WORKS.

(6.) THERE IS A CHESS AND CHECKERS PAVILION AT 65th AND 5th.

(7.) THERE IS A WORKING CAROUSEL AT 65th AND 7th.

(8.) THERE ARE TWO ZOOS.

(9.) THE DAIRY AT 65th ST. AND 6th AVE. IS THE INFORMATION CENTER.

(10.) THE LASKER RINK-POOL IS AT 106th ST. AND EAST DR.

(11.) THE WOLLMAN SKATING RINK IS AT 63rd AND 6th AVE.

(12.) THERE IS A BANDSHELL WHERE CONCERTS ARE GIVEN AT 71st ST. AND EAST DR.

(13.) BOATS CAN BE RENTED (TO PEOPLE OVER 16) TO USE ON THE LAKE.

(14.) BELVEDERE CASTLE IS THE CENTRAL PARK LEARNING CENTER.

(15.) THE URBAN PARK RANGERS LEAD WALKS AND TALKS.

22. **Q.** FIND A MAP OF NEW YORK SHOWING MOST OF THE PLACES YOU'VE SEEN.

    A. SEE NEXT PAGE.

23. **Q.** WHAT DOES MANHATTAN MEAN?

    A. IT COMES FROM THE ALGONQUIN INDIAN LANGUAGE AND MEANS "ISLAND OF THE HILLS."

24. **Q.** WAS NEW YORK EVER THE NATION'S CAPITAL?

    A. YES. FROM 1785 INTO 1790.

25. **Q.** IN 1626, HOW MUCH DID PETER MINUIT PAY FOR MANHATTAN AND WHAT IS THE MOST INTERESTING FACT ABOUT THE TRANSACTION?

    A. $24. THE INDIANS HE BOUGHT IT FROM WERE NOT FROM MANHATTAN.

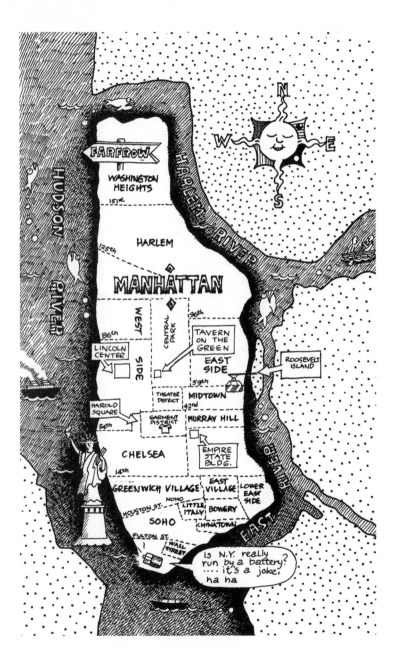

ABOUT THE AUTHOR

PAULA DANZIGER travels extensively throughout
the United States. She is tired of hearing people
say, "New York City. Gross! It's so dirty, disgusting, and dangerous."

Ms. Danziger, who has never been mugged and
has never mugged anyone, has written this book
to show how exciting New York City can be.

She is the author of several best-selling novels
for young people, including *This Place Has No
Atmosphere, It's an Aardvark-Eat-Turtle World,
The Divorce Express, Can You Sue Your Parents
for Malpractice?, There's a Bat in Bunk Five, The
Pistachio Prescription,* and *The Cat Ate My Gym-
suit.*

Ms. Danziger lives in New York City and
Woodstock, New York.